BY LAUREN ST JOHN

Wolfe and Lamb Mysteries

Kat Wolfe Investigates
Kat Wolfe Takes the Case

Legend of the Animal Healer Series

The White Giraffe
Dolphin Song
The Last Leopard
The Elephant's Tale
Operation Rhino

Laura Marlin Mysteries

Dead Man's Cove
Kidnap in the Caribbean
Kentucky Thriller
Rendezvous in Russia
The Secret of Supernatural Creek

One Dollar Horse Series

The One Dollar Horse
Race the Wind
Fire Storm

Stand-Alone Novels

The Snow Angel
The Glory

Lauren St John

KAT WOLFE
TAKES THE CASE

Farrar Straus Giroux

New York

For my niece, Alex Rheeder, who gives me hope and
inspires me to fight to save wild animals and wild
places every single day

Farrar Straus Giroux Books for Young Readers
An imprint of Macmillan Publishing Group, LLC
120 Broadway, New York, NY 10271

First published in Great Britain by Macmillan Children's Books, 2019
Printed in the United States of America
by LSC Communications, Harrisonburg, Virginia
Designed by Aram Kim and Aimee Fleck
First edition, 2019
1 3 5 7 9 10 8 6 4 2

mackids.com

Library of Congress Control Number: 2019931331
ISBN: 978-0-374-30961-9

Our books may be purchased in bulk for promotional, educational, or business
use. Please contact your local bookseller or the Macmillan Corporate and
Premium Sales Department at (800) 221-7945 ext. 5442 or by email at
MacmillanSpecialMarkets@macmillan.com.

CONTENTS

KAT WOLFE
TAKES THE CASE

PROLOGUE

Seven Months Earlier
Eastern Healing, Mayfair, London

WHEN THE LAST PATIENT HAD DUCKED out into the drizzle, Kai helped his father tidy up. He placed the acupuncture needles carefully in the sharps bin, mopped the floor, and polished the walnut cabinet that held Dr. Liu's store of traditional Chinese medicines.

Most days, he enjoyed working at his dad's practice after school. Dr. Liu was a legendary healer, renowned for the life-changing treatments he offered his adoring patients. One famous client had told the *Sunday Times* that Dr. Liu could just about "bring folks back from the dead." Kai hoped to do the same when he grew up.

Today, though, all he cared about was fighting dragons.

"*Hŭ zĭ*, I have to go out on an errand. Put *Minecraft* away and do your homework."

"Dad, I'm not your tiger cub anymore," Kai complained without looking up from his screen. "You have to stop with the nicknames. I'm almost thirteen."

"That's not how parenting works, *hŭ zĭ*. You'll still be my tiger cub when you're fifty. Put that phone down and lock the door after me. We're closed."

Kai tucked the phone into his pocket but returned to his game as soon as his father was gone. He'd summoned an ender dragon using a cheat. Now it was circling. His adrenaline spiked as it sent a plume of purple dragon's breath his way. If he could capture it, he'd be able to—

The shop bell clanged, almost giving him a heart attack. Absorbed in his battle, he half shouted, "We're closed! Come back tomorrow."

"I don't think so."

The door swung open, letting in a whiff of rain. Shiny black shoes advanced. Irritated, Kai dragged his eyes from the dragon. Dread shot through him. The owner of the shoes was masked. Black leather gloves protruded from the sleeves of his long black coat. A hat was pulled low over his eyes.

"Where's your father?"

Kai thought frantically. If he told the stranger—most

likely a robber—that his dad would be back any minute, would it scare him off or make the situation worse?

"Sorry, Dr. Liu is out. Can I help you?"

His phone was in his hand, invisible below the countertop. Glancing down quickly, he tapped nine twice. Before he could tap it a third time to summon the police, the phone was plucked from his grasp. He watched in shock as it was smashed to pieces with a tire iron.

"No more bright ideas if you want to live to see tomorrow," the stranger said pleasantly. "Now, where does your father keep the miracle cure?" He pulled open a couple of drawers in the cabinet and dashed their contents to the floor. "Don't play dumb—you know the one I mean."

Another drawer smashed, shooting pink "five-flavor" powder everywhere.

"Stop!" Fear gave way to fury as Kai saw his father's life's work being trashed by the villain. "I don't know what miracle cure you're talking about. If you're sick, make an appointment. I'm sure my father can help you. He's the best."

The man gave a dry laugh. "We know he's the best. That's why I'm here."

The door jangled and Dr. Liu walked in, shaking an umbrella. "Can you believe it, Kai, I forgot my wallet." He froze, taking in the ransacked drawers, the masked stranger, and the tire iron. "What's going on! *Hǔ zǐ*, are you hurt?"

"Nobody's hurt, and if you have the good sense to cooperate, Dr. Liu, no one will be. Give me what I need, and I'll be gone in five minutes."

Before Kai could run to his dad, the stranger, so tall that his hat brushed the low ceiling, moved to stand between them.

Dr. Liu's grip tightened on his umbrella. Thinking the better of it, he laid it down and lifted his hands in surrender. "My wallet's on the desk in my consulting room. Please take it and go."

The stranger smirked. "It's not your money I'm after, Doctor—it's your medicine. Not for me, mind. I'm asking for a friend."

"What's wrong with your friend?"

"My friend's dying, but you are going to fix that."

Dr. Liu gave a nervous laugh. "Dear sir, it appears you've been misled. I am a mere acupuncturist and herbalist." He jumped as the tire iron destroyed a tray of glass jars, sending splinters flying. Shakily he went on: "If I can assist in easing any symptoms or suffering, it would be an honor. But first I would need to see the patient."

"That won't be possible. You'll have to make do with medical records."

A sheaf of documents was slapped down on the counter. Kai noticed that every mention of both patient and physician names had been blacked out.

He tried to spot details that he could later describe to the police, but apart from his height and accent, there wasn't much to go on. His eye, skin, and hair colors were hidden by his hat, gloves, and mask, and there were no visible clothing labels or scars. The only oddity was his shoelaces—sky blue against glossy black leather.

His father scanned the medical records of the unknown patient with growing horror. He thrust them away. "What you're asking is beyond the power of any doctor! It is in the realm of the gods."

The stranger was unmoved. "Here's what's going to happen, Dr. Liu. You're going to give me your most powerful cure. On the first day of every month, you will leave a fresh batch in Hyde Park. We'll tell you where. For every month the patient survives, your son gets to stay alive. If Patient X dies, the kid dies too."

"No!"

"I'm afraid so." The intruder glanced at the clock on the wall. "We're out of time. Give me what I need or face the consequences."

Dr. Liu didn't hesitate. He went directly to an unlabeled drawer at the bottom of the cabinet and unlocked it using a key he'd told Kai was lost. Lifting out a pouch, he tipped misshapen lumps of brown, purple, and gray onto the counter.

The stranger nodded approvingly. "Is that what I think it is—*long chi*?"

"Dragon's teeth. Yes."

It was as if Kai had been parachuted into a real-life version of his game. His father selected two "teeth," crushed them into powder, and added them to a tincture of herbs, ginger, and ginseng. "Tell your . . . Tell the patient to take six drops under the tongue at the stroke of twelve, twice a day."

A black-gloved hand spirited the bottle away into a coat pocket. "Your cooperation is noted, Dr. Liu. If you value your son's life, you'd be wise to keep up the good work and tell no one about our . . . arrangement."

The shop bell tolled, and the man stepped out into the rainy dark. Kai clung to his father in a way he hadn't since he was five. Dr. Liu's heart pounded against his ear.

"Dragon's teeth?" Kai burst out. "But dragons aren't real, Dad. Those fossils in the pouch, what are they? Where did they come from?"

His father seemed to have aged ten years. "That's a tale for another day, son. All that matters is that the tincture helps his patient."

Kai felt cold to the core. "Will it?"

"There are stories . . . We have to hope they are true."

"And what if they aren't?"

His father gripped his hand. "You're going to have to trust me. I will do anything on earth to keep you safe. Anything at all."

AFTERSHOCK

Bluebell Bay, Jurassic Coast, England

"ARE YOU *SURE* THIS IS A GOOD IDEA?" asked Kat Wolfe.

"Positive," puffed Harper Lamb, struggling up the cliff path from the village. "How else would I get to see the mystery mansion I've heard so much about? Didn't you say that this is the only way up to it?"

"Yes, but—"

Kat stopped in shock as Harper suddenly tripped in the most treacherous section of the climb—the part where the railing ended and the cliff edge was exposed to the sea. With nothing to stop her, she pitched headfirst toward oblivion. Leaping to grab her best friend's arm, Kat caught a dizzying glimpse of waves foaming around the rocks in the bay far below.

"Let's come back next week or the one after that," she suggested, steering Harper to the safe side of the path and getting scratched by brambles for her efforts. "We have the whole of the summer holidays. It's not as if Avalon Heights is going anywhere."

The American girl polished sea spray from her glasses before answering. Three and a half months after breaking both legs falling off her racehorse, Charming Outlaw, she was still weak, and she tired easily. But, though her heart was pounding practically out of her chest and her long-unused thigh muscles were burning, she refused to admit defeat.

Throughout the solving of their last case, Harper had been confined to the sofa in Paradise House, the home she shared with her paleontologist father and their housekeeper, Nettie. The girls had met soon after Kat, whose mum was the seaside town's resident vet, started a pet-sitting agency to make pocket money. Harper's dad had hired Kat to exercise Charming Outlaw while his daughter was in plaster.

Around the same time, Kat had been asked to take care of an Amazon parrot then living at Avalon Heights. Harper vividly recalled Kat describing her first visit to the house. She'd clambered up the cliff path in freezing fog, only to find the front door ajar and the parrot agitated and gibbering, his owner missing. A series of strange events had convinced Kat that the bird's owner was the victim of foul play. She'd turned to Harper for help in solving the mystery. It had been the start of an adventure that had almost cost them their lives.

Today, the sky was a cheerful blue, scrubbed clean of clouds. The July sun felt toasty on Harper's skin. Even so, a chill rippled through her as she gazed up at the steel-and-glass house, its deck jutting like a clenched jaw over the ocean.

"Earth to Harper. Want to turn back?" Kat was saying.

"Why? Are you scared?"

"What? Of course not! Why? . . . Are you?"

Harper grinned. "Not today. For months, I was so creeped out by your stories about Avalon Heights that I'd have been petrified to set foot in it. But I don't feel that way now. I'm super excited. I can't wait to see if it's how I pictured it."

And with that, she set off up the final steep stretch of path, wincing but determined not to complain. Kat hurried after her. A minute later, they were on the steps of the futuristic house. A swinging FOR RENT sign screeched forlornly in the wind.

Kat rang the doorbell.

Harper stared at her. "I thought you said the place was empty."

"It is. The estate agent came into the clinic yesterday to buy puppy food. She told my mum that it's taking time to find the right tenant. I'm just checking that there's no one else here. The agency might have sent in a cleaner or handyman."

She jabbed the bell again.

Harper was now having second thoughts. "What happens if we're caught? Do you think we'll be arrested?"

"I doubt it." Kat tapped the entry code into a security panel. "Everything that made the house secret and special is gone. But it's still private property. We'd get into trouble for trespassing. We'll have to be quick. In and out. A peek is all you get. And *don't* touch anything." She frowned at the lock and tried different combinations.

A sharp gust sent another shiver through Harper. Why in the world had she told Kat that she'd die of curiosity if she didn't get to see inside the house that had figured so powerfully in their last mystery? Right now, she wished she was safely on the sofa at Paradise House. Up close, Avalon Heights had a chilly, unwelcoming air.

"I've changed my mind. Let's go."

Steel bolts snapped back. The heavy door swung open. Kat disappeared inside. Harper followed reluctantly, leaving her sneakers beside Kat's in the hall.

The minute she walked in, she forgot to be nervous. Forgot that just because the previous tenant had given Kat the door code didn't mean it was okay to use it. Forgot everything except the mind-bending house, with its all-glass front and eye-popping views. The glittering indigo sea seemed to spill in through the windows in a sunlit wave.

"Oh, Kat, it's even better than I imagined! My dream house times ten. I'd move in today if I could. Look at the home cinema and— Ohmigosh, is that a gym? Uh, what's wrong?"

Kat was at the foot of the steel staircase, staring up, her freckled face alert. She put her finger to her lips and mouthed: "Did you hear that?"

"Hear what?" Harper mouthed back.

"A sort of tortured groan."

Harper heard only the muffled crash of waves. Now that she was inside it, the house didn't seem scary in the least. "Could be a bird in the roof, or maybe the water pipes," she said, not bothering to lower her voice. "That can happen if a place has been empty for a while. Stop being a scaredy-cat, Kat, and show me around."

Harper began to twirl around the vast living room, wobbly as a newborn foal.

Kat cast one more glance up the stairs before deciding she was worrying about nothing. She skated across the polished floorboards in her socks, skidding to a halt and taking a bow. Harper danced her way into the kitchen, singing as she went.

"Careful!" Kat laughed, jumping to save a vase that Harper almost swept to the floor. "If we break something, it'll take a lot of explaining."

She peered under the breakfast bar. "Remember me telling you how I found an army-type briefcase here? I'm sure it came from a hidden compartment in the kitchen. I still have it, you know. There's nothing interesting in it. Just some old—"

There was a crash. Kat sprang up, nearly bashing her head. "Oh, Harper, what have you done?"

A shelf lined with dinosaur mugs now had a glaring gap. *Tyrannosaurus rex* was in pieces.

Harper was aghast. "It wasn't me—I promise! I was nowhere near it."

"A poltergeist did it—is that what you're saying?"

"Probably the exact same poltergeist you heard moaning and groaning upstairs," retorted Harper. "Seriously, Kat, I was standing right here when *T. rex* sprang into the air as if it were jet-propelled. But don't worry. I've seen those mugs in the deli. I'll buy one with my pocket money, and we'll figure out—"

She clutched the kitchen bench. "What's going on?"

The floor and shelves had begun to shudder. Pots clattered against saucepans, and the row of mugs clinked madly. In the living room, the chandelier tinkled like a wind chime in a gale.

As abruptly as it had started, the shaking stopped, but not before the shelf had ejected another dinosaur.

"The poor stegosaurus!" Harper poked at its shattered remains. "I love those."

Kat was wide-eyed. "Never mind the stegosaurus. What just happened?"

"Last time I felt vibrations like that was in San Francisco during an earthquake. By California standards, it was barely a blip, but I wouldn't want to go through another."

"We don't really have earthquakes in the UK—not serious ones anyway," Kat reassured her. "West Dorset had a tremor last year, but Mum says it wouldn't have cracked an egg. Maybe they're holding a parade or a drill at the military base across town? The soldiers are forever practicing blowing stuff up. If it was a big enough blast, we'd feel the aftershock."

"Up here? At the top of the cliff?" Harper looked doubtful. "Kat, what if the house really is haunted?"

"Don't ghosts prefer Gothic ruins?" joked Kat, although in truth she was spooked. She fetched a dustpan and swept up the mess. "Let's get out of here before anything else is destroyed and we take the blame."

"We can't leave before I've been out on the deck!" cried Harper. "Oh, please, Kat. That's the part I've been looking forward to most."

Kat glanced at the chandelier. The last time she'd visited, a craftily concealed CCTV camera had recorded her every move. It was gone now, but she couldn't shake the feeling that they were being watched.

"All right, but hurry." She put on her sneakers, ready to leave.

"Hurrying," said Harper, pulling on her own shoes and limping across the living room. "Moving faster than the speed of light." She slid open the glass door and stepped out onto the deck. "Wow! Double wow. Imagine filling that hot tub with bubbles and sitting there, gazing out to sea."

Kat said, "Can we go now?"

"In a second." Harper put her eye to a telescope and rotated it slowly. She took in the snaking gold line of the Jurassic Coast, the lush green fields, and the razor wire and guard towers of the army base before turning to the turquoise cove that gave Bluebell Bay its name. The pretty pastel town formed a crescent around it.

"Kat, I never knew it was possible to see the whole of Bluebell Bay. There are no soldiers on the firing range, so it can't have been a bomb drill that shook the house. And it wasn't a quake, because Edith, our favorite librarian, is chatting away to some kids outside the Armchair Adventurers' Club. None of them seem bothered. Nor do the newlyweds arriving at the Grand Hotel Majestic in their Rolls-Royce. Dad was invited to an event there last month. He says the place is spectacular, and he's normally never impressed by anything newer than a hundred million years old."

Kat was hardly listening. She wished they'd never come. "I'm counting to three, and then I'm going—with or without you."

"Okay, okay—keep your wig on." But Harper stayed where she was, transfixed by the view.

"One . . . two . . ."

"Hey, what's that?" The telescope tilted sharply downward.

"Don't know and don't care," said Kat, losing patience. "I'm leaving."

"There's a dog. I think it might have fallen down the cliff."

"A dog? Let me see! Is it hurt?"

Kat flew to Harper's side and pressed her eye to the viewfinder. A brown-and-white blur was moving behind a gorse bush on the rickety old beach steps that led from the cliff at the far side of the property to a small sandy cove. The steps, which were even steeper and more treacherous than the path up from the village, were closed to the public. Kat adjusted the focus, but the creature had lain down. All she could make out was an ear.

She leaned over the railings in an effort to get closer to the steps that zigzagged down the cliff. The minutes ticked by with no further movement. "Do you think it's climbed up on its own?"

"I'm sure it's fine," replied Harper, more with hope

than conviction. "Probably scampering around Bluebell Bay by now, stealing sausages."

A howl of pain cut through the air. From that moment on, Harper knew that nothing short of a nuclear disaster would convince Kat to leave without the dog. Nor did Harper want her to. It's just that there were two ways of rescuing it, and she was already sure that she was not going to like the Kat Wolfe way.

"Kat, wait!"

It was too late. Kat was already halfway down the fire ladder on the side of the deck. She ran along the cliff's edge and leaned past the warning sign at the top of the crumbling steps. "There it is!" she shouted over her shoulder. "Looks like a border collie. Seems to be trapped. I'm going down to try to free it."

"Are you nuts?" demanded Harper from the deck. "Those steps are closed to the public for good reason. Any second now, they might fall into the sea. And if the dog is hurt, it could bite you. What if it has rabies? Don't move. I'm on my way!"

Harper left the house via the front door and rushed to Kat's side. "Let's call your mum. She'll know what to do."

"Mum will be operating now. By the time she gets the message and calls the fire brigade or whoever, it might be too late—especially if the dog is bleeding or severely dehydrated. In emergency situations, every minute counts."

"What about Sergeant Singh?" persisted Harper. "If he's not out chasing burglars, he could sprint up here and lend a hand."

Kat shook her head. "If the dog is nervous, more people will only make it worse. Harper, these steps have been shut for years. There are whole gorse bushes and hay fields growing up through the cracks. They're not going to collapse in the next ten minutes. The quicker I go, the quicker I'll be back."

Without waiting for a reply, she squeezed past the warning sign and started down the steps. She rounded the bend and was gone.

Left alone, Harper suddenly felt fearful. What if Kat fell? Fifty meters below, the waves steamed up to the rocks with unnerving force. She tried to comfort herself with the knowledge that the cliff had stood for millions of years and survived marauding dinosaurs. It didn't help. She kept envisioning Kat being crushed flatter than a tortilla by falling boulders.

"Kat! Come back! Please, let's call the emergency services!"

Invisible, Kat responded in the calm, patient voice she used around frightened animals. "Harper, I'm close to the dog, so I'm going to be quiet in case I scare it. Don't panic if you don't hear anything."

Don't panic if you don't hear anything.

Easier said than done.

THIRTEEN SECONDS

ON THE CLIFF BELOW, KAT WAS NOWHERE near as confident as she'd made out. Even from a distance, she'd been able to tell that the collie was a stray. Its dull, matted coat stretched taut across its ribs as it struggled to its feet, growling. Dark spots of blood marked a crooked path down the steps to its present position beneath a gorse bush.

The dog was in a desperate state. Though the late-afternoon sun was still hot enough to fry an egg, the collie shivered constantly, a sign of fever and infection. Weak as it was, its hackles were raised. It was in attack mode.

Winning over animals made lethal by pain and fear was Kat's special gift, but soothing them took time, and time was not on her side. She'd have to fast-track a few dog-whispering techniques and pray they'd work before it was too late.

The steps were uneven and broken in places. The tide was high, and the sea felt disturbingly close, ready to drag Kat under if she fell. The sooner she was back on solid ground, the better she'd like it.

First, she had to prove to the collie that she wasn't a threat, which she did by sitting on the concrete and hugging her knees. She closed her eyes too. Waiting for a sign that it was safe to approach took all the patience she had.

At last, she heard it—a desperate whine.

Kat turned to find the collie, a female, lying on her side, as if her brief show of defiance had drained her strength. She barely stirred when Kat stroked her head. A silver disc on her tatty collar gave her name: Pax.

Kat blinked back tears when she saw the problem. Pax had caught her front paw in a rusty wire noose attached to a steel stake. The more she'd fought to escape, the deeper it had cleaved into her flesh.

Kat tugged at the stake, but it was embedded in the concrete and impossible to lift. She'd have to try to loosen the wire—a move that could get her bitten. Before she could attempt it, Pax surged at her with a savage snarl. Her hot breath seared Kat's cheek.

Kat reeled back, shocked. Though she'd had her fair share of nips and scratches, no animal had ever attacked her. It was only when Pax began barking that she realized the collie's fury was directed not at her but at something in the ocean.

A fiery light flared over the sea. The cliff seemed to shudder, and there was an unholy rumble, as if an ancient monster had awoken in its underground lair. Kat and Pax were flung together and shaken like popcorn. Dirt and shredded gorse stung their skin.

Then, suddenly, all was still.

Kat scrambled to her feet. On the cliff top above, Harper was screaming her name. As Pax lay dazed, Kat whipped off the noose. The collie whimpered but didn't snap at her. Swiftly, Kat bound the collie's wound with one of her socks. Now all she had to do was persuade the dog to climb forty steps on three legs before the cliff disintegrated.

"This is going to hurt, but you need to trust me," she told Pax as she helped her to her feet.

The collie's legs trembled with pain and effort, but she followed willingly enough, confirming what Kat had suspected: Pax had once been well trained and, most likely, well loved. She was a young dog. If they survived this, she might recover.

Hunger and blood loss had, however, left Pax weak.

Halfway up the cliff, she started weaving. Kat was breathless from trying to lift the collie from step to step. A hard knot of panic clamped her chest. Shale and churned-up roots kept pinging past them.

What if they didn't make it?

"I'm coming down to help!" shouted Harper.

"*No!*" Kat screamed. "Stay where you are in case you need to call the emergency services. Three on the steps might be one too many."

Harper didn't reply, and Kat knew what she was thinking: *What if* two *on the steps is too many?*

Just twenty-one more to go . . . seventeen . . . sixteen . . . fifteen . . . fourteen . . .

Pax's legs buckled, and she crumpled into a dead faint. The collie had given all she could. There was nothing left.

An image of a firefighter popped into Kat's head. If firefighters could carry towering or overweight humans using a "fireman's lift," surely she could do the same with a skinny collie. Kneeling, she slung Pax across her shoulders. Gripping the collie's front legs in one hand and her back legs in the other, Kat began to climb.

Thirteen steps. Thirteen seconds. Would it be quick enough?

Twelve . . . eleven . . . ten . . . nine . . . eight . . .

An orange life ring came bouncing down the cliff. Kat caught it and was relieved when Harper tugged the other end. "*You can do it, Kat!*" her friend encouraged. "You're *so* close!"

Seven . . . six . . .

Kat paused. Her thighs felt as if they were being chargrilled by flamethrowers.

"Don't you dare give up!" screamed Harper. "Your mum needs you! Tiny needs you! *I* need you!"

Five . . . four . . . three . . .

Harper grabbed her arms just as a crack split the last concrete step at the speed of a striking snake. One final heave, and girl and dog were on the cliff top.

Kat scrambled to her feet. "Run! Run for your life!"

It wasn't possible for either of them. She was carrying the collie, and the most Harper could manage was a fast hobble.

When at last they were a safe distance from the edge, they looked back. Immediately, they felt silly. Nothing had changed. Avalon Heights was still standing. So were the cliff steps. There'd been no landslide or any other natural disaster.

Far below, Bluebell Bay basked sleepily in the sunshine: Tourists window-shopped and sipped lattes, kids played Frisbee on the harbor front, and the park was packed with picnickers.

"Was any of the last hour real, or was I hallucinating?" asked Harper. "At one point, I thought I saw a humungous shark swimming past the cliff."

As she spoke, a seagull rose screeching from the roof of Avalon Heights. The cliff gave a soft, almost human sigh and snapped off like a broken biscuit, plummeting into the sea. A bloom of white foam was all that marked its passage into the depths.

The girls stared after it, stunned.

Until that moment they'd managed to persuade themselves that what they'd done, though extremely risky, had not actually been life-threatening. Seeing the sea swallow the steps Kat and Pax had just climbed and the cliff edge Harper had been leaning over left them under no illusion that they wouldn't have been swallowed up too.

Harper stammered: "Y-you were just . . . I could have . . . *We* nearly *died*."

"Yes, but we didn't," Kat said firmly. "That's what counts. We're still here and breathing." She hesitated. "Do you think we should say anything to my mum or your dad?"

"Are you kidding? No! I mean, they'd only worry, right?"

"Right. Why cause a fuss when we're safe and sound." Kat shuddered. "In future, remind me to stay away from creepy empty houses."

"And crumbling precipices," agreed Harper.

Kat soothed the collie, who was beginning to come to. "It'll all be worth it if we can save Pax. I think I saw a wheelbarrow behind the house. If we use it as a stretcher, we can get her to the animal clinic in record time. Just don't mention where we found her."

"Don't worry, it's erased from my memory," muttered Harper, knowing, even as she said it, that this was purely wishful thinking.

HISTORY IN THE MAKING

WHEN THE MACHINE-GUN CLATTER OF helicopter blades woke Kat the next morning, her first, hopeful thought was that the Dark Lord might be swooping in for a visit.

It wasn't hard to see how her grandfather—aka Lord Hamilton-Crosse, the government's minister of defense—had come by his nickname. Whenever he appeared on the news, his falcon face and unforgiving gaze tended to reduce even hard-boiled interviewers to stuttering imbeciles. Reporters forgot their questions. Opponents melted into blobs of dismay. Then there was his job, which was shrouded in secrecy. From what Kat could gather, her grandfather had enemies the length and breadth of the country.

For a long time, he and her mum had been on opposite sides too. When Kat was born, he'd refused to accept that she was the daughter of his late son, Rufus, who'd died while surfing a giant wave. He'd turned up at the maternity ward and accused Ellen Wolfe of being a gold digger desperate to get the billion-pound fortune of the Hamilton-Crosses in her clutches. Anything further from the truth was difficult to imagine, yet it had taken him eleven years to admit he was wrong, and longer still to say sorry.

Had Kat and her mum not moved to Bluebell Bay, their paths might never have crossed again. Fortunately they had, because when Kat and Harper's first investigation turned deadly, he and Kat had saved each other. More than that, they'd developed a grudging mutual respect. Not that either of them would ever dream of admitting it.

"See you when I see you, Kat Wolfe," the Dark Lord had said vaguely when they'd last met, in the spring.

"Not if I see you first," Kat had quipped.

At the time, she hadn't thought he'd heard her. Now she wondered if he had. Certainly, she hadn't seen him since. That was the trouble with kidding about caring. You didn't always get a chance to take it back.

She knew from the newspapers that, in recent months, he'd made a number of official visits to the nearby army base. Never once had he dropped in at 5 Summer Street for so much as a cup of tea. Yes, he was busy and important, but it still hurt. And last week, a long-promised weekend at Hamilton Park, her grandfather's famous stately home, had been postponed yet again hours before they were due to leave.

"Don't take it to heart, honey," Dr. Wolfe had implored, giving Kat a hug. "Your grandfather's dying to see you. It's just that, as usual, the prime minister has forced him to cancel his plans. If it's any consolation, your grandfather has promised to make our stay extra special when it does finally happen."

It didn't take Sherlock Holmes to deduce that Dr. Wolfe had invented the last part, but Kat loved her mum for trying to let her down gently and for choosing to believe, despite all evidence to the contrary, that the Dark Lord was full of warm, grandfatherly thoughts. Dr. Wolfe always saw the best in everyone—even him.

The helicopter was back and had now been joined by a second. They whirled so close to Kat's attic bedroom that Tiny, who'd been purring on her chest, stripy tail swishing, flew into the wardrobe at the speed of a cheetah on the scent.

When Dr. Wolfe had applied to manage the Bluebell Bay Animal Clinic, a condition of the job was that the Wolfes adopt Tiny, an F1 Savannah cat requiring a wild animal license. A traumatic kittenhood had left him scarred. It had taken a great deal of love and patience for Kat to win his trust. Even now, strangers and loud noises terrified him. All Kat could see of him was one green eye glaring through a crack in the wardrobe door.

"Why is a BBC News helicopter trying to land in your garden?" Harper asked plaintively from the sofa bed, startling Kat, who'd forgotten she'd stayed over. "How's a girl supposed to get any sleep?"

"BBC News?" Kat sprang off her futon, belatedly discovering that the exertions of the previous day had left her feeling as if she'd been pummeled by grizzly bears. She sat down, head spinning. It all came rushing back then: the collapsing cliff, the race against time to get Pax to the animal clinic, and the relief of watching her mum's skilled, tender hands stitching up the collie and administering antibiotics and fluids. Pax had spent the night in the clinic kennels recovering from her ordeal. Kat couldn't wait to see her.

She recalled something else: the fiery light she'd seen arc across the sea, like a rocket launcher, and the shadow of an immense shark, spotted by Harper. Pax must have seen it cruising the shoreline too. Was that why she'd barked with such ferocity?

As the helicopter did another flyby, Harper's phone made music in her rucksack. She fumbled for her glasses. "What is this—Grand Central? It's the crack of dawn on

Sunday. Is Bluebell Bay on fire? Have aliens landed on the roof of the Armchair Adventurers' Club?"

Kat giggled. "Oh, I hope it's an invasion of little green men. We need a new mystery for the holidays."

She opened the window and leaned out into a sparkling morning. The two helicopters were now circling the beach. A crowd was gathering near the harbor.

A terrible thought occurred to Kat. What if someone had been attacked by the shark Harper had seen skulking in the depths?

The largest marine predator ever spotted on the Jurassic Coast had turned out to be an innocent eight-meter basking shark, hungry for plankton. But what if a great white had swum into town? How would Bluebell Bay cope with its very own *Jaws*?

Before that thought could pick up speed, Harper interrupted by passing over her phone. "Look at this message from Dad."

Hey, kid. Want to be part of something historic? Get yourself to the beach PRONTO. Don't even stop to brush your teeth. Tell the guards that you and Kat are my assistants.

"What guards?" asked Kat. "Does he mean life-guards?"

Harper was pulling on shorts and a sweatshirt. Her face was alive, sleep forgotten. "All I know is that my dad's the most laid-back man in the universe. If he says to get to the beach in a rush, we should fly. If history's being made, I want to be there. Don't you?"

FIND OF THE CENTURY

THEY RACED DOWN TO THE HARBOR ON their bikes, pausing only—at Kat's insistence—to check on Pax in the kennels. She was asleep, bandaged paw twitching as she dreamed.

"You'll be glad to know she's doing beautifully," said Tina Chung, the veterinary nurse who lodged with the Wolfes. "Better still, we've found her microchip. We'll reunite her with her owners as soon as we can. They'll be thrilled to have her home."

Kat tried to feel thrilled too, but couldn't quite manage it. She was already in love with Pax, who was named after the goddess of peace, and had been secretly hoping that the collie could stay with them forever. As she and Harper cycled through the streets of Bluebell Bay, Kat told herself off for being so selfish. If Tiny were lost and some other girl found and decided to keep him, she'd be devastated. It was right and proper that Pax should be returned to her own family. Kat knew she would just have to get over it.

The girls skidded to a halt near the sailing club. All thoughts of the collie went from Kat's head as she took in the scene. The caramel sands of Bluebell Bay—often teeming with dog walkers even at this hour on a Sunday—were empty, glistening, and extra wide, as if the sea had been instructed to roll back and stay there.

But it wasn't the sight of an uncrowded beach that had the town residents gawking on their doorsteps in curlers and pajamas. The tide had been at its highest at around midnight. The effects of the landslide had become evident only as the waves retreated in the early hours of that morning.

At the edge of the beach, a police cordon manned by two security guards in black T-shirts held back a buzzing wall of phone-clutching onlookers. A posse of sweaty cameramen kept bashing the unwary with their heavy lenses. In the parking lot beyond, Sergeant Singh was remonstrating with the driver of a *Fast News* broadcast van, while a TV reporter with confident blond hair was having her lipstick touched up.

Spotting a gap in the crush, Harper dived in. Kat wriggled after her, wrinkling her nose at a musky armpit. They were brought to a halt by a man mountain. Kat's gaze traveled up and over a hillock of chest, then up some more. Atop the mountain was a pair of dark sunglasses.

"No kids on the beach," barked the guard. "Not unless you want your skull cracked open by a boulder. In case you hadn't noticed, half the cliff's collapsed into the bay. The only people allowed into the cove are dinosaur experts with hard hats and photo ID."

"Paleontologists, you mean," Harper said brightly. "That's why we're here. We're Professor Lamb's assistants."

He snorted. "And I'm the Easter Bunny. Move along. You're in the way."

Harper didn't budge. "We won't be in the way if you let us through. That's Professor Lamb down at the far end of the beach. He's Bluebell Bay's official paleontologist, and he needs our help urgently."

"Doing what, exactly? Building sandcastles? Hold on, sir . . ." The security guard stuck out a tattooed arm as a gaunt man tried to sneak past. "The beach is closed until further notice."

"Says who? I've been fossil hunting here since I was knee-high to a crab. I know my rights. Let me go." The man made a dash for it, nearly knocking Kat over. There was a jam stain over his heart.

"They're the ones you should be stopping, not me," he ranted, stabbing a finger in the direction of Professor Lamb and his group. "Call themselves experts? They don't have a clue."

"Harper and Kat?" A young man in an Indiana Jones–style fedora came rushing up. "Phew, I thought I'd never find you. It's bedlam here, and that's *before* we've announced an official discovery. The rumor mill's working overtime." He stuck out a tanned hand. "Ollie Merriweather. I'm a PhD student from Bristol Uni. I'm working with Professor Lamb for the summer."

He handed them hard hats. "Hurry, guys. I don't want to miss the big find—if there's one to miss. My thesis is riding on this." He nodded at the guard. "It's cool, Mike—they're with me."

But as they set off along the beach, Jam-Stain Man swerved around the guard and seized Ollie's arm. "You tell Professor Lamb that if the reports are true, he doesn't understand what he's unleashing. When blood is spilled, as blood will surely be, don't say Harry didn't warn you."

There were titters from the crowd. Ollie grinned as Mike steered the man away. "I'll do that, Harry. Thanks for the tip. Come on, girls—let's go."

"What was that about?" demanded Harper, struggling to keep up with the student's long stride. "I don't want Dad mixed up in anything dangerous."

Ollie laughed. "Trust me, you have zero worries on that score. Ask any paleontologist or archaeologist, and they'll tell you that nutters are a hazard of the job. Whether we're in Tutankhamen's tomb or Timbuktu, no discovery is complete without some local crackpot gabbling on about the forces of ancient darkness and blood being spilled."

"How does Harry know what you've found if you haven't found it yet?" asked Kat.

The student slowed. "At daybreak, a fisherman noticed a mysterious shadow on the exposed cliff face and put it on social media. Every fossil fanatic in the United Kingdom seems to have seen it."

"What mysterious shadow?"

A helicopter blasted overhead, and Ollie covered his ears. "We've asked the coast guard to keep the choppers away from the cliff so they won't blow any fossil we do uncover to Antarctica, but it's had no effect."

They found Theo Lamb balanced on a stepladder, examining flecks in the sandstone. Before she'd met him, Kat had pictured Harper's father as tweed wearing and eccentric, with "mad professor" hair. In fact, he was as easygoing as he was brilliant. His mop of brown curls gave him a boyish demeanor, and he was almost always in faded jeans and a band T-shirt. Today it was Bob Dylan.

He waved from the ladder. "Hey, assistants! Good to have you here. Stay well back unless I tell you to approach. This cliff's as fragile as powdered sugar."

He returned to studying the sandstone while Ollie and seven or eight other Jurassic Coast experts and officials spread out along the beach, necks craned, scanning the rock for hints of bone.

Harper was fizzing with anticipation. "Kat, this could be it—*the* find that makes his name. For years, Dad's been trying to convince his paleontology peers that Bluebell Bay's cove hides a sleeping giant like Predator X. That's the biggest ichthyosaur ever discovered. That's why we moved to the Jurassic Coast from Connecticut— so he could hunt for it. He's been called a clueless know-nothing more times than I can count. Now he has a chance to prove his critics wrong."

The urgency of Professor Lamb's text message had led Kat to believe that a dinosaur skeleton would be unveiled shortly. But nothing happened for an exceedingly long and boring time. Every now and then, the stepladder was shifted and various people tapped at rocks with geology hammers while others shook their heads. The sun climbed higher. Kat was both starving and yawning. She began to feel quite cross.

She took off her shoes and stood in the shallows, staring up at the cliff. What had caused the vibrations that she and Harper had experienced before it collapsed? Did they have a natural or unnatural cause? Had anyone else noticed them?

"Ladies and gentlemen, girls, thank you for your patience," said Professor Lamb, climbing off his perch.

"I'm sorry to disappoint everyone, but it seems we've been the victims of an elaborate hoax. As Jonathan Swift said, 'falsehood flies, and the truth comes limping after it.' That's what we're looking at here: fake news, Jurassic-style."

Groans followed this announcement. One by one, the experts drifted away, heading back into town.

Harper threw her arms around her father. "It's not fair, Dad. I was hoping so much that this was going to be the find of the century for you. I could cry with disappointment."

He ruffled her hair. "No tears, kiddo. That's the way it goes sometimes. You gotta be philosophical in this business or you lose your marbles. How about I treat you and Kat to brunch?"

A BBC helicopter thundered overhead, peppering them with grit. He raised his voice. "DAMN THESE CHOPPERS. LET'S GO EAT WAFFLES."

"Professor, wait!"

Ollie's arm was arrow straight. He was pointing at a bulge in the sandstone about three meters above him. The crumbling gold rock gave the illusion that something was twitching beneath it, like a sidewinder viper emerging from a desert dune. Professor Lamb's face went the mauve of a Chesil Beach pebble. He grabbed Harper's hand, and she grabbed Kat's, and they moved forward together, as if in a trance.

A film of gold dust lifted off the cliff face. Kat had

the sense of a billowing curtain being blown back. The sunlight caught the bleached bones beneath, turning them silver.

Ollie clutched at his hat. "Tell me I'm not seeing things."

Harper said faintly, "A dragon!"

"And not just any dragon," said her father. "If I'm not mistaken, it's a two-hundred-*million*-year-old dracoraptor, breathing fire across the ages. It's so perfectly preserved that one could almost believe it capable of springing from its sandstone tomb to hunt again."

Kat's heart skipped a beat. Her eyes met Ollie's. Amid the excitement, there was something distracted in his, as if he were remembering the earlier threat—the one he'd laughed off and forgotten to pass on.

Tell Professor Lamb that . . . he doesn't understand what he's unleashing. When blood is spilled, as blood will surely be, don't say Harry didn't warn you.

GHOST ROOMS

"MA'AM, I'VE CHECKED THE RESERVATION system three times. Unless we have a ghost wing I'm not aware of, we're fully booked. *Over*booked, to be truthful."

The woman's husband slid a fifty-pound note across the reception desk. "Any chance we can persuade you to search harder for one of these, uh, 'ghost' rooms?"

"*Sir*, even if an invisible room were available, which it's not, it's against hotel policy to accept bribes . . . and pets," said the manager, staring coldly at the French bulldog the couple was trying to conceal behind a suitcase. The man's smile could have frozen a polar bear.

At the Grand Hotel Majestic, Kat and Harper had spent an entertaining afternoon watching these exchanges from the comfort of a blue velvet sofa under the overhang of a luxuriant palm. It was free theater.

Dinosaur hunters, reporters, and travelers from as far away as Rajasthan and Cancún competing to cajole, berate, and bribe the manager into giving them rooms at the best hotel on the Jurassic Coast, most to no avail. The couple from Yorkshire were just the latest casualties of his arctic politeness.

Kat almost felt sorry for them. Almost, but not quite. Didn't they read the news? Had they spent the past three and a half days in an undersea cave? How could they not know that ever since Professor Lamb and Ollie Merriweather had unearthed one of the oldest and best-preserved dinosaurs ever found in the United Kingdom, Bluebell Bay had become the center of the paleontology universe?

Every fossil obsessive, newshound, or wannabe documentary maker who could fly, drive, or crawl to the Jurassic Coast was here. The narrow lanes were gridlocked, and with half the beach still cordoned off, the town heaved. There were queues outside every restaurant, including the Sea Breeze Tea Room, which everyone knew made the driest scones and most execrable tea in all of Dorset.

The farmers were making a fortune renting out their fields to campers, and there'd been so many fights over parking that extra police had had to be drafted in from Bridport.

And still the hordes kept coming. Some arrived half

expecting to find the dracoraptor already excavated and cantering along the beach like a CGI dinosaur from the movies. Most came to get as close as possible to what the tabloids were calling the "Jurassic Dragon."

"Despite appearances, it's not a dragon as such," Professor Lamb had told the BBC lunchtime news. "In some people's minds, the fiery dragon of myth and lore was, or evolved from, an actual dinosaur. I can assure you that it's a creature of fantasy, pure and simple."

"But isn't it true that when the first dracoraptor was discovered in 2014, it was named after the Welsh Red Dragon?"

Professor Lamb's mouth twitched. "Yes, but that's because Nick and Rob Hanigan, the amateur paleontologists who discovered it in the Vale of Glamorgan, wished to honor the national symbol of Wales. *Draco* is Latin for 'dragon,' and *raptor* means 'robber' or 'plunderer.' What *we've* found is a carnivorous neotheropod. A distant cousin of *T. rex*. She's a new species of dracoraptor— as agile as a leopard, with serrated, daggerlike teeth for slicing through flesh. We know that she roamed these shores around two hundred million years ago during the Hettangian age of the Early Jurassic—"

"If the dinosaur you found is not a dragon, how do you explain the wings on her shoulders?" the presenter broke in.

"Excuse me?"

An image of a dragon-shaped shadow on Bluebell Bay's distinctive cliffs flashed up behind Theo Lamb.

"This photo, taken by a fisherman on the morning of the find, clearly shows what some are saying is the first evidence of the real-life flying reptile that inspired the mythical dragon. Do you think you might be mistaken about her being a dracoraptor?"

"What you're seeing is a trick of the light. Behind the dracoraptor, we found a trace fossil of a pterosaur—"

"You're saying there was no flying creature on that cliff?"

"We are not in a position to confirm or deny, but—"

"We're out of time, Professor Lamb. Thanks for your insights."

Harper watched the interview five times straight on her phone, becoming more annoyed with each viewing. "Most reporters aren't interested in science, only sensation. The find on its own is miraculous. Why do they need some fantastical angle?"

Kat was still gripped by the parade of hopefuls to and from the front desk. "You have to admit that even you thought it was a dragon when you first saw it . . ." She moved a palm frond to get a better view. "Oh no! Another poor family just crashed and burned."

As the family fled, dragging a drooping cockapoo, Harper prodded Kat. "Now's your chance. Go give the manager your Paws and Claws Agency business cards."

"No way! You heard what he said about pets. What's the point in leaving pet-sitting cards around when none of the guests are allowed animals?"

Harper rolled her eyes. "Because it's a once-in-a-lifetime golden opportunity! Over the next few weeks, everyone who's anyone will be visiting the Majestic. They won't just come to stay. They'll come to wine, dine, and network. Some of those winers and diners will have dogs that need walking or kittens that need company. You wanted new riding boots. This is your passport to paying for them."

Harper's dimples deepened. "'Course, if you'd rather spend the summer sifting through dracoraptor bones with me and Dad . . ."

Kat smiled. "Thanks, but no thanks." Much as she adored Harper and Professor Lamb, the thought of spending hours at a stretch dusting off dinosaur ribs when she could be racing Charming Outlaw along a beach or cuddling kittens was not appealing.

She took a bundle of Paws and Claws cards from her rucksack. "Right, I'm going in. If I'm not back in five minutes, send a search party."

"Will do," confirmed Harper. "Give me some cards. I'll scatter them around. Good luck with the manager. You'll be fine as long as you avoid eye contact. It's the icicle stare that gets them every time."

* * *

First stop was the hotel library. Harper left five Paws and Claws cards on a glass table piled with Belgian-chocolate-coated strawberries. HELP YOURSELF! a pink sign invited her. She nibbled a strawberry thoughtfully while studying a framed poster of Agatha Christie's *Death on the Nile* and wondering whether she and Kat should have business cards printed for Wolfe & Lamb Incorporated. How else would they find a new mystery to solve?

Next, she visited the garden. The Majestic occupied a commanding position on the slopes above Bluebell Bay, and its terraced lawns, blooming with red roses and blue rhododendrons, were as famous as its pool.

Bending to trail her fingers through water the hue of crushed aquamarines, Harper studied the guests baking on white lawn chairs. Despite their plush surroundings, none seemed relaxed. One man clutched his phone so tightly to his ear that the blood had drained from his knuckles.

Two umbrellas along, a pale freckled man with a pale freckled partner was taking delivery of a watermelon carved into the shape of a shark. Its black grape eyes were as enigmatic as the man's sunglasses. Each time he spoke to the woman, he covered his mouth with his free hand, as though afraid that the waiter or a fellow sunbather would read his lips.

On the opposite side of the pool, Rosalyn Winter,

blond TV reporter for Fast News, frowned over her laptop, typing furiously. She'd been in Bluebell Bay since the morning of the discovery.

A familiar hat caught Harper's eye. Its wearer was in the terrace restaurant, on the top tier of the garden, obscured by a jungle of hydrangeas. Harper ventured closer, discreetly dropping Paws and Claws cards on Rosalyn Winter's table and two garden benches. There was no mistaking the fedora owner's eager voice.

"I can't thank you enough for trusting me with this assignment. You can count on me, I promise."

A chair scraped back. Ollie Merriweather came striding jauntily across the lawn. Harper glimpsed his table companion's hairy wrist as its owner replaced a green-and-gold bottle in an ice bucket. Had Ollie been drinking champagne too? In the short time she'd known him, he'd mentioned the size of his student loan three times.

His grin turned lopsided when he saw her. "Harper! What are *you* doing here?"

"I was going to ask you the same thing," said Harper, noting that he'd swapped his rumpled chinos and polo shirt for a crisp white shirt, smart vest, and tie.

"What am *I* doing here? I, umm, ran into an old friend." His gaze raked the garden. "Is your father with you?"

It occurred to Harper that her dad might not approve

of her and Kat scouting for pet-sitting business at the town's fanciest hotel. "No, I'm helping a friend."

"You mean Kat? I think she's trying to get your attention."

Through a thicket of pool umbrellas and climbing roses, Harper saw Kat waving wildly. She lifted a hand in response.

Ollie leaned nearer. "Maybe don't mention you saw me here, eh, Harper? Wouldn't want your dad to think I was slacking off. I'll be working late tonight to make up for it." He winked. "No harm in helping a pal."

Whistling, he exited through a garden gate. Before joining Kat, Harper glanced at the terrace table he'd vacated. A waiter was shaking out a fresh white cloth. Ollie's "friend" had gone.

STARSTRUCK

POOLSIDE, ROSALYN WINTER SET DOWN
her laptop, snatched up a robe, and sprinted along the
path that led to reception. A buzz hummed through
the garden. Deck chairs were upended as other guests
followed. A waitress abandoned a tray of smoked salmon
sandwiches to the seagulls. Harper joined the slow-
motion stampede.

"What's going on?" she asked as Kat tugged her word-
lessly behind a pillar in the crowded but hushed lobby.

All eyes were trained on the main entrance. The
glass doors slid open and a woman glided in. Backlit
against the sky and sea, she was momentarily visible only
in silhouette, but Harper had no trouble identifying
Alicia Swann, Oscar-nominated actress and one half of
Hollywood's most celebrated couple.

Setting a leopard-print tote bag on the front desk,

the actress swept off her sunglasses. "I have a reservation for a double room, although a suite would be preferable, if you have one."

"I'll see what I can do, Mrs. Swann," simpered the manager. "It's my great pleasure to welcome you to the Grand Hotel Majestic."

But, as he scrolled down his screen, he didn't look pleased. He looked perplexed, then panicked. Though he tapped busily at his keyboard, it was clear to the girls, standing nearest him, that the booking was either lost or had never been made. Kat suspected the latter.

She was intrigued. Would the manager send one of the world's best-loved actresses packing? Or would he conjure up a "ghost" room, perhaps by booting out another guest?

"Apologies for the delay, Mrs. Swann. I'm having trouble locating your reservation."

She gave him a smile that could have refloated the *Titanic*. "Take your time, Mr. Karlsson."

"Call me Viktor!"

"Thanks, Viktor. I'll play with Xena while I wait."

On hearing her name, a fluffy red teddy bear of a dog popped out of Alicia's tote bag. The manager reeled back in horror.

"Wait till he tells her they don't take pets," an onlooker stage-whispered, earning a death glare from Viktor Karlsson.

Alicia turned on the manager. "You don't take miniature Pomeranians?"

"Ma'am, we have nothing against Pomeranians per se," he said unhappily. "It's a matter of hotel policy. Health and safety, and all that. If it were up to me . . ."

She laughed. "But it *is* up to you, Viktor! Besides, my husband and I are here only for a week or so, and my warrior princess will be spending most of her time in doggy day care. It'll be as if she doesn't exist. You *do* have doggy day care here in Bluebell Bay, don't you, Viktor?"

The blond reporter stepped forward. "Rosalyn Winter, Fast News. Delighted to meet you, Mrs. Swann. I'm pleased to say that there is a first-class doggy-day-care service here in town." Like a gambler unveiling an ace, she presented the actress with Kat's Paws and Claws Agency card.

Harper gave Kat a shove, and the manager's desperate gaze fell on the girl he'd coldly dismissed not ten minutes earlier.

"First-class doggy day care," he agreed. "And by chance, the proprietor is right here. This is, uh, uh . . ."

"Kat Wolfe," finished Harper. "The best pet sitter in Bluebell Bay!"

"Kat Wolfe? How charming," murmured the actress, scrutinizing Kat. Up close, her fragrant dark hair and high bronzed cheekbones were even more exquisite. "Aren't you a little young to be pet sitting?"

"Experience is more important than age," Harper assured her. "Kat uses the Trust Technique. Check out her website. I designed it, and it's packed with glowing references. Kat's mum, Dr. Wolfe, is the town veterinary surgeon. Her credentials are impeccable. Kat's, that is."

Alicia Swann was amused. "Are you Kat's manager?"

Harper grinned. "Kind of."

"She's precious. I'll take care of her—if it would help," Kat said. The Pomeranian was in her arms, washing her face.

The actress cried out in surprise. "How did you do that? Xena always snarls and snaps at strangers. Draws blood frequently too."

"Kat speaks Dog," Harper informed her. "And Cat, Horse, Hedgehog, and Parrot. She's a multilingual Dr. Dolittle when it comes to animals. She leaves the Latin, French, Spanish, and Mandarin Chinese to me."

The glass doors parted, and a couple came in wheeling suitcases. They had the relaxed air of people with a confirmed booking. Viktor Karlsson locked gazes with the concierge, who raced to head them off. Catching the look, Kat predicted, correctly, that they would be informed there'd been a flood or fire in their room and dispatched to some far-flung bed-and-breakfast.

"Thank you, Viktor," purred Alicia Swann as he handed her a key for the ocean-view suite. "I had a feeling this would work out beautifully."

He grimaced. "My pleasure, ma'am. Now about the dog. We can't allow—"

She laid a manicured hand on his arm. "Viktor, I almost forgot. Ethan, my husband, will be needing livery."

"Livery, ma'am?"

"Stabling. You know—for his horse." As the manager gaped, she turned to the Fast News reporter. "Thanks for your assistance, Rosalyn. If I can repay it with an interview—"

A high-pitched whinny sounded outside, followed by a scream, a crunch of metal, and the unmistakable clatter of hooves. The glass doors of the lobby slid open. One of Hollywood's best-known action stars came bounding up the steps, leading a black horse, which seemed to have pranced off the silver screen and into fiery life.

As the mare moved, her satin coat danced with blue light, and her crinkled mane flowed like silk from her high, proud head.

Ethan Swann grinned at the startled faces before saluting his wife. "Sorry, darling. Traffic was hell. Any luck finding livery?"

The actress turned to the manager, but Viktor, who was petrified of horses, was hiding under the desk.

Harper said hurriedly, "Mrs. Swann, there's no livery in Bluebell Bay, but there *is* a spare stall at Paradise House, where I live. Your horse would be welcome to use it for a week or two. I'd need to check with my dad—he's the paleontologist who discovered the Jurassic Dragon, as the newspapers are calling it—but I don't think he'll mind."

"If you need a groom or someone to exercise your horse, I'd be happy to help with that too," volunteered Kat.

"Kat's the best horse whisperer in town!" added Harper, in case there was any doubt.

Alicia Swann laughed. "But of course she is, and I'm sure the horse will enjoy her vacation at your 'Paradise' stable too. Well, then, consider yourselves hired."

A TINY PROBLEM

"I HAVE GOOD NEWS AND BAD NEWS," SAID Dr. Wolfe. "Which would you like first?"

Kat was on the kennel floor cuddling Pax, who'd recovered enough to hop around joyfully when her rescuer walked in. Seeing the collie she'd saved looking so bright-eyed and alive was all the reward she needed for risking her neck on the cliffs.

Kat had come straight to the animal clinic from Paradise House. The heavenly scent of horse still clung to her T-shirt. She liked it. It reassured her that the past couple of hours had really happened. She'd been asked to take care of a film star's horse. That was remarkable in itself. Had Ethan Swann asked her to groom and exercise an old nag, she'd have been ecstatic. Instead, she'd been entrusted with the care of a mare of near-mythical beauty—a Friesian on loan from Pet

Performers, a company that hired out trained creatures of all varieties for use in films.

Friesians were a Dutch breed of horse, and the mare's name, Orkaan, meant "hurricane." Kat assumed it was a reference to her storm-black coat, because there was nothing remotely tempestuous about her. When a frenzied crowd had gathered outside the Majestic to beg for selfies with Ethan and his horse, Orkaan stayed cool and collected throughout.

She'd also been loaded without fuss into the horse trailer that had brought her to Bluebell Bay. The actor had been joking when he claimed to have ridden her through the traffic. His Wild West entrance had been exactly that.

Harper had been over the moon at the prospect of Alicia Swann popping in for tea at Paradise House whenever Ethan took his horse for a canter. And Kat had been equally excited about introducing the actor, who'd played a racehorse trainer in his last film, to Charming Outlaw. Sadly, Orkaan and the girls had been accompanied to her holiday lodgings only by Roy, the driver from Pet Performers.

"But don't you want to check out the stable to make sure it's suitable for her?" Kat had asked Ethan, unable to hide her surprise. In *Fire Racer*, his character would never have dreamed of sending his horse to stay with a stranger without first inspecting the stall.

The actor looked astonished at the suggestion. "Have a heart, girl! My wife and I have been traveling for eighteen hours straight from LA via London. We're dizzy with jet lag. We're here for a rest. If we don't get some beauty sleep, we'll be fired from our next picture when we get back to Hollywood! Roy will see to my horse. I'll check on Orca tomorrow when I take her out for a ride."

"Orkaan," Roy reminded him.

"Right. I'll text when I'm on my way over—Kat, is it? Kat, it would be great if you could have the horse saddled and ready to roll at around ten A.M. Thanks for helping out. Keep a tab of what we owe you, and we'll settle up when we leave." His smile sparkled. "No hidden charges, now. We're not made of money!"

He was borne away on a tide of autograph hunters, leaving Harper to direct Roy to her home. Professor Lamb, who was busy with the dracoraptor, had given his approval by phone. All that remained was for Charming Outlaw to give his.

Paradise House was a red-brick cottage with roses around the door. Roy parked the horse trailer at the orchard gate. While Harper went to ask Nettie for some sandwiches and cake to offer Roy, Kat led the black mare through the apple and cherry trees to the stable yard.

Charming Outlaw came tearing up to the field gate at a racehorse gallop. He skidded to a halt with a piercing whinny. Thanks to Kat's influence, his manners had improved considerably, but he'd always be exuberant. Kat liked him that way. Beneath his naughty exterior, the chestnut was one of the sweetest-natured horses she'd ever met.

Orkaan was a film star in her own right, so Kat was careful to keep plenty of distance between her and Outlaw when she introduced them. Despite a few squeals from the chestnut and indignant snorts from the mare, she was sure they'd get along fine. Roy helped her make up the spare stall for Orkaan with a bed of shavings, fresh water, and an evening feed. He was a man of few words, but seemed satisfied that the Pet Performers' mare would be in safe hands.

Accompanying him back to the trailer, Kat plucked up the courage to say, "I'm a big fan of Ethan's film *Fire Racer*. Have you ever seen him ride? Is he brilliant?"

Roy chortled. "Real life's not like the pictures, girl. They're a funny bunch, actors. Don't go confusing them with their characters. Some are better; some are worse. One thing's for sure, they're not the same."

Roy's remarks came back to Kat as she put clean bedding and water bowls in the kennels that evening. Was Ethan better or worse than his character in *Fire Racer*? She knew she'd soon find out.

Kat had been hanging around veterinary surgeries since she was a toddler, and there were few things she enjoyed more than watching her mum work and helping out where she could. This evening, she was preparing kennels for new patients, as well as checking on others. She took time to give each poor cat and dog some love and attention.

"If an animal has been through a traumatic experience or is recuperating from a major operation, a kind word and just knowing that someone is rooting for them can do wonders for their recovery," her mum often told her. "It's not only humans who need to know they're loved."

Job done, Kat went to sit with Pax. Kat's mum, who was short, blond, and smiley, was moving from kennel to kennel, checking temperatures and dressings and administering antibiotics. It was while she was changing the collie's bandage that she said, "I have good news and bad news. Which would you like first?"

Still elated after meeting the Swanns and their dream horse, Kat opted for the bad news.

"As you know, we've been struggling to reach Pax's owner," said her mum. "Today we learned that he died recently, leaving Pax in the care of his daughter, an oil-company executive. She's claiming the collie ran away, but I suspect that poor Pax was dumped on the roadside. The daughter is refusing to pay a penny of Pax's veterinary bill and wants her rehomed. She says she's allergic to dogs."

"That's awful!" cried Kat, while secretly considering

it the best possible news. Not the part about the rich daughter having a heart of stone and refusing to pay her bill, but the bit about Pax needing a new home. In Kat's mind, that brought Pax one paw closer to moving into 5 Summer Street.

"Yes, it is, but I'm confident we'll find her a new family," said her mum. "Meanwhile, try not to get too attached to her, darling. You know we can't adopt a dog."

"You said something about good news," Kat reminded her, eager to change the subject.

"Ah, yes. All eight of our dog kennels are full, and I'd like to free one up in case of emergencies. Since Pax is on the mend, I thought you might enjoy having her stay in your attic room for a few days."

"*My* room?" Kat couldn't see how this was good news. "Not the kitchen or the living room?"

"No, it has to be your room. Too much coming and going in the others. It'll take Pax a while to recover from her ordeal. If she panics, she could run into the street and get hurt. Locked in your attic, she'll be safe and able to do *some* exercise, but not too much."

"But what about Tiny? He'll have a fit."

"Then you'll need to have a word with him." Dr. Wolfe's mind was already on her evening surgery. "I have complete faith in you, Kat. You're the best cat whisperer I know."

* * *

Ordinarily, Kat considered her mum's compliments on her animal-handling skills to be the ultimate praise, but these were not ordinary times. By the following morning, she'd have done anything to be able to hand the World's Best Cat Whisperer baton over to someone braver, smarter, or more fluent in Feline.

As feared, the cat-collie experiment had been an unmitigated disaster. Kat had done as her mum suggested and "had a word" with Tiny. She'd reminded him that, not so long before, he too had been unwanted and that now he was worshipped and pampered to within an inch of his life, and it wouldn't hurt him to extend a paw of friendship to a homeless and suffering fellow creature.

Sadly, the only paw Tiny extended had needle-sharp claws on the end of it. After a nightmarish chase and wrestling match, he'd flown out the high window, leaving Kat and Pax bleeding and enough fur on the floor to stuff a mattress.

As luck would have it, Dr. Wolfe and Nurse Tina had spent the entire evening at the clinic doing an emergency operation, which meant that Kat didn't have to confess to being a failed Tiny whisperer. Nursing stinging scratches, she'd eaten an almond butter sandwich in her room and comforted Pax, who was bewildered and whimpering. The collie couldn't understand what she'd done wrong. She'd only tried to be friendly.

By bedtime, Tiny still wasn't home. Though Kat

had gone into the garden in her pajamas and called and called, there'd been no answering meow. She'd lain awake for hours, fretting. From the moment she and Tiny had bonded in the spring, three months earlier, he'd never spent one night apart from her.

She'd prayed that Tiny would be curled up in the crook of her legs when she awoke. Instead, Pax was in his place, looking sheepish. The collie belly-crawled the length of the duvet and snuggled under her arm, tail thumping.

"You're adorable, and I wish we could give you a forever home," Kat told her. "But first, you'll need to convince Tiny it's a good idea. He's as scared as you are, I promise. If you can do that, I'll go to work on Mum."

After feeding Pax and changing the dressing on her paw, Kat went in search of the Savannah cat. He wasn't in the garden, so she crossed the street to the animal clinic. There was a wooded area behind the kennels where he liked to stalk butterflies.

As she approached, a black-haired man bounded up the steps of the veterinary surgery and leaned on the bell as if an animal's life depended on it.

"The clinic doesn't open till nine," said Kat. "I can call Dr. Wolfe if you have an emergency."

He trotted over in muddy hiking boots. "Thanks, miss, but it's not the vet I want. It's the pet sitter, Kat Wolfe. I was told I could find her here."

"You can! You have! I'm Kat."

His chiseled face, creased with anxiety, smoothed in an instant. "Pleased to meet you, Kat. My name's Rossi—Mario Rossi. I'm in Bluebell Bay to do a coasteering course. I'm going to be out every day exploring sea caves and rock hopping and cliff jumping, and I'm worried about my pet, Simon, being left on his own. Any chance you can take care of him for a week or so? Maybe longer—maybe shorter. I'll pay you up front for a fortnight."

He took a fistful of cash from the inside pocket of his jacket. "Will this be enough?"

Before Kat could answer, he added another twenty pounds and pressed it into her hand.

"Thanks, but that's way too much." Kat tried to give it back, but Mario wouldn't hear of it.

"If you keep Mr. Bojangles happy, it'll be worth it."

"I thought his name was Simon."

"Simon? No, it's Mr. Bojangles. Like the song."

"What song?"

He smiled. "A song from my youth. Now you'll need to drop in on Mr. B for at least half an hour a day. Play with him or take him for a short walk. He loves a change of scenery. It's when he gets bored that things go wrong. Keep Mr. B away from anything small and furry. I'll leave feeding instructions. It's quite straightforward.

After the last incident, I decided to go with frozen food. Safer all around."

He handed her a key card with a tiger on it and jotted his contact details on the back of a train ticket. "Thanks, Kat. You're a lifesaver. I hope the two of you get along. A lot of people misunderstand Mr. B, but always remember he has a good heart."

"That's what I say about my cat, Tiny," Kat told him. "I'm not sure anyone believes me."

He pointed his pen at her. "Are you one of those timid pet sitters who can cope only with kittens and hamsters? If that's true, you'll be of no use to Mr. Bojangles. None at all."

"I'm not a timid pet sitter," Kat said indignantly. "My mum's a vet, and I've been around animals all my life. I like the challenging ones best of all. It's a sign of intelligence."

His shoulders relaxed. "If that's your attitude, you shouldn't have a problem. Any questions, give me a call." And with that, he jogged off down Summer Street.

Kat was about to count her windfall when Tiny crept meowing from under a bush. He was bedraggled and skittish, his leopard-patterned fur standing up on end. She wondered where he'd been. He allowed her to carry him home, but it took a lot of loving and treats before his confidence returned. She left him washing himself on a sunny windowsill in the living room, restored to his old self.

Upstairs in her room, Pax had made herself at home on the futon. Kat was glad that she hadn't been foolish enough to attempt to reintroduce Tiny to the collie. As she petted the gentle collie, it struck Kat that Mario hadn't mentioned Mr. B's breed. It mattered, because some types of dogs are more unpredictable than others.

Stuffing the tiger key card and bundle of cash under her mattress, she texted Harper.

A man just offered me a crazy amount of money to babysit his "misunderstood" dog. Should I do it or not?

The reply was instant.

"Misunderstood" could mean mad, bad, or sad. When something seems too good to be true, it pretty much always is.

NOT IN THE JOB DESCRIPTION

"TWO CAPPUCCINOS AND TWO FRIED EGG sandwiches, as requested," said Harper, setting a cardboard tray on an upturned crate and handing her father and Ollie a couple of warm foil-wrapped parcels. Her own breakfast was a hot chocolate and a banana nut muffin.

"Thanks, Harper." Professor Lamb took a grateful gulp of coffee. "No offense to Ollie, but you're my favorite assistant ever."

"None taken," said the student, demolishing his sandwich in two bites. He wiped runny egg from the corner of his mouth and gave Harper a thumbs-up. "Thanks, mate. Top stuff."

Theo Lamb said mildly, "Oliver, my late wife and I named our daughter after one of America's greatest novelists for a reason. I'd appreciate it if you'd call her Harper."

Ollie reddened. "Yes, of course, Prof. Sorry, Harper. No offense."

"None taken," said Harper, forcing a smile. It was her first day of working on the dracoraptor find, and she didn't want to start out on the wrong side of the student. All the same, she was suspicious of him. When she had a minute, she planned to find out the name of Ollie Merriweather's lunch companion. It was possible that the restaurant booking had been made under the name of his friend—the friend who'd trusted him with some mysterious assignment. And if the restaurant receptionist refused to help, she might just have to hack into their website.

It never entered Harper's head that penetrating the Grand Hotel Majestic's cybersecurity system might pose a challenge. Coding and languages were her special gifts. She hadn't always appreciated them. There'd been times during their last investigation when she'd felt positively feeble just sitting on the sofa with her laptop while Kat pursued, or was pursued by, dangerous villains in the real world.

But Kat always insisted that there were different kinds of bravery. Harper knew now that her own skill set—honed by her mentor, Jasper, a hacker who helped the FBI—had been as vital as Kat's when it came to cracking the case.

Today, though, her main focus was the dinosaur. Thanks to the combined efforts of her father, a

Natural History Museum team, and a couple of British Army engineers, the block of sandstone containing the dracoraptor had been cut from the hollowed-out cliff and transported to the old rowing club on the harbor.

The hall was musty and, courtesy of the next-door fish market, had a distinct odor of cod. But at least the dinosaur was safe from the sea. For now, that was all that mattered.

Whatever Harper's misgivings about Ollie, there was no doubting his passion for his subject. He was like a kid at Christmas as he helped her father lift the protective sheet off the dracoraptor. Harper felt the same way. Waiting to see the Jurassic Dragon again was as magical as watching the curtain go up on a Broadway play.

She hadn't been able to stop thinking about how alive the beautiful little dinosaur had seemed when she first glimpsed it, as if it were already free of its sandstone tomb. In its day, it had been a leopard- or cheetah-type creature, quicksilver fast, with a long tail and steak-knife teeth. In death, it appeared to be in mid-pounce.

It also appeared to have wings, which is why it so strongly resembled a dragon. However, those wings were not attached to its skeleton, but rather a trace fossil on the slab of limestone to which it was attached.

Expecting to see both now, Harper was bewildered when the raising of the sheet revealed blocks in protective jackets. Then she remembered that sections of the skeleton had been covered in plaster molding to protect it during the excavation. The Jurassic Dragon had been cut from the cliff, together with the rock that encased it, and some five hundred kilograms of it were airlifted to the hall by helicopter. In the coming weeks, Professor Lamb and his team would peel off the jacket and use scrapers, knives, and dental picks to dig through the sandstone to the bones underneath.

As the professor unfurled a high-resolution life-sized poster of the dinosaur, Ollie said: "Prof, are you sure it's just a coincidence that the wings of some pterosaur or other flying reptile seem as if they're sprouting from the dracoraptor's shoulders? What if we're wrong and they belong to our dinosaur? What if it's another species entirely?"

"You mean like the *Zhenyuanlong suni*, the winged dinosaur found in China in 2014?"

"Exactly!" Ollie enthused. "Or the *Beibeilong sinensis* dinosaur—'Baby Louie'—that made the cover of *National Geographic* a couple of decades back. They call it the 'Baby Dragon of China.' It was a cassowary-type thing that laid eggs the size of monster-truck tires."

Professor Lamb smiled. "Ollie, as romantic as it is to think that we've uncovered a unique winged dinosaur, I'm certain that when the rocks are carbon-dated, we'll learn that these are separate species that lived millions of years apart."

"Or we might learn that a monsoon or mudslide struck just as our Jurassic Dragon was stalking a pterosaur," countered the student. "Or maybe the pterosaur was dive-bombing our dinosaur to stop it from stealing its eggs or killing its young."

"That really *would* be a coincidence" was Professor Lamb's cutting response. "I'm sure it would put you on the cover of *National Geographic* if fame's your aim, Ollie."

Harper was taken aback. It was so unlike her father to be sarcastic. The sleepless nights must be catching up with him. He was under immense pressure to do everything perfectly. Every five minutes, some expert from the University of Cambridge or Outer Mongolia was on the line offering unsolicited advice or criticizing his methods.

Even as she thought it, his phone rang again.

There was no caller ID, and Professor Lamb hesitated before picking up. Harper was alarmed to see the color drain from her dad's face. "Sorry, sir—wrong number," he snapped, switching off his phone as if it had suddenly become red-hot.

"You've been getting a lot of those crank calls, huh?" probed Ollie.

Sensing that her father didn't want to discuss it, Harper changed the subject. "It's like an icebox in here, Dad. Thanks for reminding me to wear a fleece. It's hard to believe that it's summer outside—or that the Jurassic Coast was once like a Caribbean paradise!"

Her father laughed. "It's true that it was tropical, but it was hardly a paradise."

And with that, he and Ollie immediately forgot their differences as they launched into a favorite topic of many paleontologists: the extreme conditions endured by dinosaurs.

Between them, Theo Lamb and the student painted such vivid pictures of life on Earth in the days of the dracoraptor that Harper had no trouble picturing it hunting among the forests and lagoons. Back then, the warm seas of the Jurassic Coast had teemed with life. In water often blood-red with plankton, porpoise-like ichthyosaurs had glided through coral reefs busy with lobsters, starfish, and sharks. More lethal still were the plesiosaurs—giant crocodiles that were the mega-predators of their time.

Inland, the dracoraptor would have been dodging the allosaurus and herds of diplodocus thirty-meter-long sauropods weighing twenty-thousand kilograms. Harper couldn't get her head around the amount of lush fern forests and cycads they must have munched through as they roamed the landscape like Boeing 747–sized lawn mowers.

"The common myth that dinosaurs were lumbering failures of evolution, extinct because they were too big and too stupid, is just that—a myth," said Professor Lamb. "They survived for millions of years by adapting to cope with volcanoes, megamonsoons, fearsome predators, deserts . . ."

Ollie was staring out the window. "Prof, those protesters are back. Some of their placards make me laugh." He read one out loud: "'Go away! Stop destroying Bluebell Bay!' As if *we* made the cliff fall to bits! My personal favorite is Harry Holt's sign. It's covered in fake blood and reads, 'Let sleeping dragons lie.'"

"The only way to win over the doubters is to keep doing what we're doing to the best of our ability," Professor Lamb said. "And that's what we're going to do, Ollie—our very best. Let's get to work."

He began selecting tools and instruments as reverently as a surgeon preparing to perform an operation. His team would use an air-powered engraver and medical instruments such as small scalpels to separate the rock from the bones, one grain at a time. Cracked and broken bones would be glued using an eyedropper. Slicing through the plaster with a cast cutter—the same sort doctors used to take casts off broken legs—would create a virtual sandstorm of dust, so a dust extractor was primed and ready to suck it up. The floor had been spread with oily sand and sawdust to help absorb some of the fine grit.

"Harper, while Ollie and I begin the laborious

process of investigating a two-hundred-million-year-old mystery, you get to do the fun stuff in a dingy back room. Just what you always wanted to do with your summer holidays, huh? Ready to search for buried skeletons—oops, I mean, treasure?"

She giggled. "Ready, Dad."

By midafternoon, Harper looked as if she'd run the Marathon des Sables across the Sahara. Despite spending hours up to her elbows in beach sand and rubble and filling four cardboard trays with waste rock, she'd barely made a dent in the stack of sandbags that lined the room. They'd been hastily salvaged from the foot of the cliff before the tide came in. Using a pneumatic air scribe tool, which was shaped like a pen but had a pointed, vibrating tip with air pulsing from it, Harper had been able to shave, cut, and blow scraps of sandstone or dirt away from potential fossils.

It was slow and grubby work, but Harper enjoyed it. It was somewhere between treasure hunting and detection. Over the summer, experienced adult volunteers would sift through the rubble from the foot of the cliff for any bits of bone, teeth, or claws that might provide clues to the life and habits of the dracoraptor. Until they arrived, she had the place to herself.

Her dad stuck his head around the door. "Harper, love, I have to go to Wool station to pick up a couple of volunteers, and Ollie's off to get sandwiches. Are you all right on your own, or would you like to come with me? You're quite safe here. Mike's guarding the gate."

Harper, who had headphones on and was practicing Mandarin Chinese while she probed at lumps and rocks with a fossil incisor airbrush, mimed that she wished to stay.

After he'd left, she kept thinking about the unwelcome call her father had received. It hadn't been a wrong number; she was sure of it. What had the caller wanted? And why had her father reacted so strongly?

A breeze lifted her hair, as if someone had entered the adjoining hall. Harper took off her headphones. "Dad, is that you? Did you forget something?"

There was a scuffling and skittering of claws. Rats. The dilapidated building was overrun with them. Harper made a futile attempt to clean her glasses. With each bucket of grit and grime, the world had become blurrier. She didn't mind mice, but if one scampered her way, she'd prefer to be able to see it.

Standing up to stretch, she saw through the cracked window that the security gate had been left unguarded. She spied Mike leaning against a fence post some way off, chatting up a pretty girl. Harper was annoyed. An entire team of dinosaur thieves in stripy burglar suits could have strolled past and he wouldn't have noticed.

Judging by the footsteps suddenly echoing around

the hall, the burglars were already here. Before Harper could react, there was a volley of yaps in the passage. A Pomeranian came flying into the room, leash trailing.

"Come back, you minx!" shrieked Rosalyn Winter, tottering in after it. She was startled to see Harper. "What are *you* doing here?"

Harper eyed her coolly. "I belong here. I'm helping my dad. What are *you* doing here? Mike's not supposed to let anyone in."

The Fast News reporter scoffed. "If the professor wants to keep the dinosaur safe, he might want to employ a guard with a brain bigger than a walnut. Anyhow, I'm only here because I'm trying to track down Wolf Girl. Until I do, I'm Xena's doggy day care, and I'm not happy about it, I can tell you."

She held up a thumb encased in a bloody bandage. "Don't try giving that red menace a treat. This is the thanks you get. If I have to have a digit amputated, I'm going to sue Alicia Swann for her home in the Hollywood Hills."

Harper giggled. "Sorry, I don't mean to laugh, but it's hard to believe that Alicia's adorable little bear could hurt a flea." She smiled indulgently at Xena, who was sniffing at the heap of sandbags. "If you don't like Mrs. Swann's dog, why are you looking after her?"

Rosalyn plunked herself in Harper's chair. "I keep asking myself the same question. One minute, I was about to film an exclusive interview with Alicia in her suite at the Majestic. Next, she received a message requiring her to drop everything and dash. She was so sweet and apologetic, I didn't have the heart to be upset when she asked if I'd mind taking 'darling Xena' to her 'dear friend Kat Wolfe.' She didn't warn me that Miss Cutie-Chops was a rottweiler in Pomeranian clothing. Where is Wolf Girl? I was told I might find her here."

"Kat's coming over as soon as she's finished pet sitting," said Harper. "You're welcome to leave Xena with me until then."

"That's kind, but what if you get bitten? And won't the professor mind?" Rosalyn cast a critical eye over Harper's appearance and the fossils in a bowl on the table. "What the devil does he have you doing? You look like the loser in a mud-wrestling competition."

Harper couldn't decide if Rosalyn was bracingly rude or refreshingly honest. "Not that it's any of your business, but I'm searching for buried dinosaur treasure. Fragments of bone or teeth or claws. Anything that might help Dad piece together the life of the Jurassic Dragon."

"If that's what you're up to, then Xena's your ideal assistant! We've been here for all of three minutes, and she's won the bone lottery."

The Pomeranian's teeth were fastened around a mottled beige object poking out of a sandbag. She was tugging at it with all her tiny might, snarling like a saber-toothed tiger. As Harper braved a nip trying to get her to drop it, the bag split, ejecting something heavy.

It hit the tiles with a crack and rolled under the table, grinning ghoulishly as it went. Harper grabbed Xena's leash to stop her from going after it.

"I'm no expert," drawled Rosalyn Winter, "but that's no dinosaur."

TAILS OF THE UNEXPECTED

AT THAT EXACT MOMENT, KAT WAS CYCLING through Bluebell Bay and trying to process a morning beset with unsettling events.

First, she'd had to deal with Tiny going missing and returning looking as if he'd been mauled by a sea lion.

Then Mario Rossi had made her uneasy with his eagerness to hand over three times her normal fee for taking care of a pet, which, he'd informed her, ate only defrosted food after some undisclosed incident. *Safer all around*, he'd said. Kat regretted not pressing him on the matter.

Breakfast had been interrupted by an emergency call from a nearby farm. "A lamb has been mauled by an unknown creature," Dr. Wolfe had told Kat when she got off the phone. "'Sheep worrying,' they call it. Every farmer's nightmare."

"Fox or dog?"

"It was dark, but Chris Carmichael thinks neither." Her mum looked over at Tiny, sleeping with one green eye open on the windowsill. "He believes it was a huge spotted cat."

For ten tense seconds, they both stared at the Savannah cat. Dr. Wolfe didn't ask if Tiny had an alibi for the previous night, and Kat didn't tell.

Ellen Wolfe picked up her veterinary response bag. "Like I said, it was dark, and the sheep were milling about. Could have been a zebra for all Chris knows. I'll keep you posted. Have a good day, honey."

Next on Kat's pet-sitting agenda was the horses. As she pedaled through the country lanes to Paradise House, she convinced herself that Tiny was innocent. No question. He was big enough to pounce on a three-month-old lamb, but she couldn't imagine him doing it even if he was starving. It's not that he wasn't capable of lashing out if he felt threatened, as he had when Pax invaded his space, and Kat made the mistake of getting between them. But that was rare. Beneath his mean and moody surface, he was supremely gentle. Kat had never known him to harm so much as a sparrow. He chased butterflies. That was the extent of his hunting prowess.

Even so, there was no denying he had been missing overnight. Kat planned to keep him locked in the house that evening, no matter how much he complained. She didn't want anyone seeing him out wandering and falsely accusing him.

At Paradise House, she groomed the horses and schooled Charming Outlaw over a few jumps. The Swanns had promised to text her at around 10 A.M. to confirm Ethan's visit to the stable and Xena's doggy day care, but by midday, she'd heard nothing.

Kat didn't mind waiting. It gave her an excuse to spend more time with Orkaan. She sat on the stable floor with Hero the calico cat on her lap, reading a mystery novel out loud. The black mare's dark eyes never left her. Friesians were renowned for being fiercely loyal to people who were kind to them, and Kat was keen to build a strong rapport with the horse.

Five chapters later, she gave up on the Swanns. They'd probably found an older, more glamorous pet sitter and would have their agent call her later to break the news.

She was pushing her bike through the orchard when a high-pitched cackle frightened the birds from the cherry trees. "'Your money or your wife? Which is it going to be?' 'Your money or your wife? Which is it going to be?' 'Your money or your wife? Which is it going to be?'"

Kat had no difficulty recognizing the screechy voice of Harper's adopted yellow-crowned Amazon parrot. His previous owner had loved action films, and Bailey loved shouting out quotes from them. However, it was the first time that the actor who'd originally spoken the lines finished the parrot's sentence for him.

"'Forget it—I'll take both!'" she heard Ethan Swann say.

Another cackle. "'FORGET IT!'" shrieked Bailey. "'I'LL TAKE BOTH!'"

Kat abandoned her bike and ran up the garden path. To her astonishment, the actor was standing in a flower bed looking through the Lambs' partly open living-room window. What on earth was he doing? He hadn't made an appointment to ride, and, apart from Kat, there was no one in. Harper and her dad were at the harbor with the dinosaur, and Nettie had popped out to the farmers market.

There was something so intent and focused about the way the actor stared into the room that Kat felt a flutter of nerves, though she doubted he was casing the joint. That would be ridiculous. Ethan Swann was a Hollywood star. It was unlikely that he spent his holidays burgling humble country cottages, especially in broad daylight while wearing cowboy boots.

As if to prove this, there was no trace of guilt or embarrassment in Ethan's expression when he saw Kat. He didn't even climb out of the flower bed. He simply crinkled his ice-blue eyes.

"Hey there, Kat the cat sitter! Do you live here?

Whoever's in that room sounds like he has one of my movies stuck on repeat."

Kat laughed. "That's only Bailey. He's my friend Harper's Amazon parrot. He loves action films and must have seen one of yours." She pointed as Bailey flapped into view, alighting on a skeleton. "That's him there, on top of the dinosaur. Harper's father's a paleontologist. He's the one who discovered the Jurassic Dragon last week."

"Professor Lamb? Yeah, we heard about the great discovery." Ethan leaned through the window again. "Is that the magic dragon that's been in the news? Shouldn't it be in a glass case with an infrared alarm on it or something?"

Kat stifled a giggle. "That's a different type of dinosaur, and it's only a model. The real dracoraptor is under twenty-four-hour guard at the harbor."

"Oh, sure, I thought it was too easy. Out here in the middle of nowhere." Impatiently, he shook his corn-colored bangs from his eyes. "Good to know the real dragon's safe."

Kat had no idea what he was talking about. She wondered if he was a trifle dim. Just because he'd played a neuroscientist in *Saving Billy* didn't mean he was brain-surgeon bright in real life. "Would you like to see the stables?" she asked. "I've turned Orkaan out, but I can saddle her up for you, no problem."

Ethan followed her to the field, where he made her day by insisting that if he'd been aware of Charming Outlaw's existence prior to filming *Fire Racer*, "We woulda cast this fella instead. You say he's fast?"

"On the track, he was nicknamed the Pocket Rocket," Kat said proudly.

Though he'd come dressed to ride, the actor told Kat not to bother fetching a bridle. He seemed agitated, as if he couldn't wait to get away. "The GPS led me astray on the way here, and now I'm all outta time. Alicia and I have plans. I'll take Orca for a spin another day."

"Orkaan," Kat said automatically.

"Right."

At the gate, she watched him fire up a silver Aston Martin V12 Vanquish.

He leaned out the window. "So long, Kat. I'll be in touch."

The sports car sped off along the leafy country lane, growling like a discontented tiger. As Kat collected her bike, a puzzling detail popped into her head. If it was impossible to miss hearing the Aston Martin go, why hadn't she heard it arrive?

MR. BOJANGLES

TWENTY MINUTES LATER, KAT WAS CY-cling along the coastal path, still puzzling over the actor's behavior. Mario Rossi was staying in the RV park and campground near Durdle Door, a natural limestone arch that always reminded Kat of a horse bowing its head to drink from the sea. Beyond it was Man o' War Bay. She'd spent many joyous hours racing Charming Outlaw along its caramel sands.

She paused there to do some deep breathing. Getting into a positive state of mind was important. If Mr. Bojangles *did* turn out to be a slavering pit bull, Doberman, or rottweiler, it was critical that he didn't scent her fear.

Mario's motor home was parked at the far end of the holiday village. It was twice the size of its neighbors and had a sleek, dark-gray chassis and blacked-out windows. As she slid the tiger key card into a silver slot, Kat was encouraged by the silence. Any decent guard dog would have been baying at the door by now. Either Mr. Bojangles wasn't as temperamental as Mario had made out, or he was a heavy sleeper.

The door hissed open. Cautiously, Kat stepped inside. The first thing she noticed was the temperature. Perhaps because he hailed from the sunny Mediterranean, Mario liked his home on the hot and humid side.

Kat wriggled out of her sweatshirt and stared around in mild awe. The place was wall-to-wall chrome, with black and cream fittings. On a foldout walnut desk, a laptop screensaver scrolled through striking photographs of elephants, tigers, beluga whales, and rhinos. A high-end audio and video setup took up one wall. Noise-canceling headphones were curled over a hook.

There was no evidence of any living animal. No squeaks, tweets, snuffles, meows, or growls.

"Mr. Bojangles?" Kat called softly.

The silence was more unnerving than a snarling German shepherd would have been. At least then she'd have known what she was dealing with. This way, her imagination went directly to panthers and piranhas. Beasts with big teeth and claws—and a taste for pet sitters.

What if Mr. B wasn't a dog at all? Come to think of it, Kat realized, Mario had only ever talked about his "pet." Then there'd been the confusion over his name. She'd thought he'd said "Simon." What rhymed with Simon? Lion? Scorpion? Bison?

And what type of animal inspired such a grand moniker as Mr. Bojangles? Was he a cat with issues, like Tiny? Or something exotic—a monkey, say? Kat scanned the tops of the cabinets. Was he hiding somewhere, ready to pounce?

Or did she have the time wrong? Could Mario have taken his poodle, ferret, or alligator out for a walk? No, that didn't make sense. He'd hardly have paid her a fortune if he'd been around to entertain Mr. B himself.

The galley kitchen smelled of garlic, sun-dried tomatoes, and fresh basil and pasta. Kat found that comforting. On the counter was a note.

Hi, Kat,
Thanks for taking on Mr. B at such short notice! Don't worry about feeding him. He's a fussy eater, and it's easier if I do it. Have fun!

Mario

While Kat was relieved not to have to deal with Mr. B's defrosted food, it also meant that she couldn't rely on a bag of coley fish, for example, to provide clues as to his species. She was beginning to think he must be a hamster, skink, or leopard gecko kept in a cage or tank. That would explain why he hadn't greeted her.

She crept around the motor home like a spy on the prowl. There was nothing furry amid the sofa cushions, and no tanks or cages near Mario's workstation or in the shower stall. Two yacht-style cupboards looked promising. One was locked. Kat investigated the other, but it too was a pet-free zone. The only item of interest was a box on a low shelf containing a brand-new helmet, wet suit, and buoyancy aid.

Kat was surprised. Mario had told her he was doing a coasteering course. If that was true, why hadn't he taken his protective gear? He'd need it if he planned on cliff jumping, rock climbing, and swimming in dangerous sea caves. But perhaps he was only a beginner, learning basic skills on dry land before attempting the cliffs and deadly currents of the Jurassic Coast.

She moved into Mario's bedroom, where she was horrified to see a snakeskin cushion propped against the pillows. Kat loathed people who considered wild-animal parts to be fun home accessories, and she decided at once to return the man's money and sack him as a client. He could find some other sap to take care of his mystery pet!

Mind made up, she redoubled her efforts to locate Mr. B. She couldn't leave the creature lonely, or his cage or tank grubby, just because his owner had terrible judgment.

At the foot of the bed was a black-lacquered cabinet covered by a cloth printed with dragons. Gingerly, she lifted a corner. Beneath it was a glass-fronted vivarium— the type that housed snakes and bearded dragons. It was decorated with a grapevine and live greenery. Bark chips and newspaper lined its floor, and a large water bowl sat in one corner. The fact that there was a heating pad at one end and a cool area at the other suggested it might be home to a python or boa constrictor. The lid was askew, leaving a gap.

Kat glanced at the bed and her pulse rate tripled. The snakeskin "cushion" was gone! And she'd thought Ethan was dim!

When her phone vibrated in her pocket, Kat practically levitated with fright. If it was Mario, she was going to tell him off for failing to warn her that his pet was an escape-artist python.

Or was she? Here was a once-in-a-lifetime opportunity to hang out with what she guessed was a royal or ball python, so named because they curled into a tight ball if they felt threatened. Rather than being cross with the Italian, she should thank him for trusting her with Mr. B.

She flipped open her phone. The Dark Lord was calling.

Kat was stunned. Not a word from her grandfather in months, and he deigned to ring now, while she was on her hands and knees attempting to gauge from a safe distance whether there was a snake under the bed. Much as she liked pythons, it was disturbing to have one on the loose in a strange motor home. She'd have let the call go to voicemail if she'd thought he'd bother to try again this side of Christmas.

"Hi, Grandfather." She kept her tone casual, as if they chatted every day.

"Katarina, thank goodness I've reached you. How are you? That is to say, are you safe and well?"

"Totally safe and extremely well. How are you?"

"I, er, look, it's daft, really. I just had a sixth sense you needed urgent help."

Kat got to her feet, mouthing "Ohmigod" at her phone. How did he intuit these things? It was uncanny. "Ha, that's funny! No, everything's okay in Bluebell Bay," she lied. "Thanks for checking. I'm just, you know, busy pet sitting."

He sounded relieved. "Anything interesting?"

"The usual. Cats, dogs and— Eek!" Something cool had brushed against her ankle.

"Did you say eels?"

In the split second it took Kat to react, a five-foot-long royal python whipped its coils around her ankles, binding her legs together. "Exotic p-pets, I mean. S-some people have them."

"Nothing deadly, I hope."

Mr. Bojangles tightened his grip. Kat let out a squeak. "Hope not!"

"Kat, are you sure you're being truthful? You're not in some kind of difficulty?"

"I'm a bit tied up, that's all. Nothing I can't handle."

"I'll be brief then. I was wondering . . . That is to say, if it's acceptable to you and your mother . . . and if you've not made other plans . . . I'd love you both to come to Hamilton Park for the weekend. I have horses."

Kat was finding it hard to concentrate. The python thought she was a tree. Or dinner. He squeezed lovingly. Then not so lovingly. Kat lost the battle to stay upright. Toppling backward onto the bed, she lay there like an upended beetle, her legs in the air, snake still attached. His coils were cold and unexpectedly heavy.

There was an edge to the Dark Lord's voice. "Look, I've obviously caught you at a bad time. Talk it over with your mother. If you don't wish to visit, I'll understand."

Kat's stomach muscles contracted as she reached for the tip of the python's tail. If she could get a firm grip, she could unwrap him. The snake drew back his head to strike, tongue flickering. Pythons aren't venomous, but they have four rows of teeth at the top of their mouth and two rows on the bottom and can inflict a nasty bite. Slowly, so as not to alarm Mr. B, Kat withdrew her hand.

"But I do wish to visit," she said breathlessly into the phone.

"You do?"

Royal pythons had a reputation for being gentle, curious pets, unless they'd been ill treated or wild-caught, in which case all bets were off. Kat hoped Mario was right about his python's good heart. She smiled up at the snake, picturing her grandfather's face if he could see her now. "I'd love to stay at Hamilton Park. And meet your horses."

"Excellent. The invitation extends to your friend Harper Lamb too. She's most welcome if it's something she'd enjoy."

"Thanks, Grandfather. Harper's helping her dad with the Jurassic Dragon, but I'll check if she's free. Did you hear about Professor Lamb's big find on the news?"

The line crackled.

"Grandfather? Grandfather, are you there?"

The snake hissed irritably.

"Be careful, Kat," the Dark Lord said at last. "These things have a habit of stirring up strong passions in unscrupulous people. I wouldn't want you to get in the way of them."

The python was squeezing again; Kat's feet had gone numb. "Sorry, Grandfather—I have to go. The pet I'm sitting is threatening to eat me if I don't play with him."

He laughed. "Well, I wouldn't want that. Tell your mother I'll be in touch about the weekend. And Kat . . ."

"Yes, Grandfather?"

"I hope you're aware that if you ever are in trouble, I'm here for you."

He hung up without waiting for a response. Kat tossed her phone aside and devoted all her energy to unwrapping the python. Thankfully, it was easily done now that she had both hands free.

Grateful to have escaped being bitten (likely) or crushed (unlikely), she set about cleaning the vivarium and changing the water. Despite their shaky start, she was confident that she and Mr. B would become friends. She liked his adventurous spirit.

Her phone rang from the folds of the duvet as she was draping him over his grapevine. Securing the vivarium lid, she dived for it. "Hey, Harper."

"Kat, I have to be quick because Sergeant Singh's pulling up outside, blue lights flashing. You're not going to believe what we've found. Not me exactly, but the dog. Kat, she found . . . She found—" Harper broke off, too distressed to continue.

"You're scaring me, Harper. Slow down. Breathe. Which dog? What have you found?"

"A skull . . ."

"Another dinosaur skull?"

"A *human* skull! Alicia's Pomeranian dug it up."

"A human *skull*!" Kat couldn't believe her ears. "How did Alicia's Pom get the chance to dig up a skull? Are there bodies buried under the patio at the Grand Hotel Majestic? Or is it an ancient head—a Roman soldier or something?"

"Long story and, no, that's what's so upsetting. It's too soon to say how or when the person died, but Dad thinks it might be the male victim of a cliff fall in Bluebell Bay two years ago. We found the skull mixed in with the rocks and fossils from the beach."

The hairs stood up on the back of Kat's neck. She'd come within a whisker of being crushed by rocks herself. "Harper, I'm on my way. I'll be there in ten minutes, max. And don't worry. If there's any mystery about this skull, we'll solve it together."

She pulled the dragon cloth over the vivarium, ignoring the snake's baleful gaze. Dragons and skeletons. They were everywhere.

DEATH BY MISADVENTURE

"WOULD ANYONE LIKE A CRUMPET WITH coconut cream and maple syrup?" asked Edith Chalmers, head librarian at the Armchair Adventurers' Club, on Friday morning. "They're well-known for combating nerves."

"Thanks, but no, thanks," said Harper, sinking into a beanbag. "It doesn't seem right to eat when a man has died."

"*Ages* ago, according to your dad," Kat pointed out, putting two crumpets on a plate and flopping down beside her best friend. "That doesn't make it any less sad, but I doubt he'd mind if we had breakfast."

Edith settled on the sofa beside Toby, her golden retriever. "Your consideration and compassion are admirable, Harper, but it's also important to keep up your strength. If Sergeant Singh and the coroner have uncovered a suspicious cause of death overnight, we may have a new mystery on our hands."

Harper hid a smile. When Kat had begun dog walking for Edith not long after moving to Bluebell Bay, the retired school librarian had been "on the shelf," as she herself put it. Isolated and frail, she'd faced a future devoid of thrills in a soulless, cabbage-scented retirement home.

What everyone, including her own son, had lost sight of was that Edith had a librarian's encyclopedic knowledge and radical gifts. For much of her seventysomething years, she had been stepping boldly through the portal of the pages in her library to climb Everest, outwit smugglers and assassins, sail the high seas, hike the Silk Road, swim with dolphins, and dance *Swan Lake*.

Rounding the world in eighty days was all in a day's work for her. Naturally, she'd learned a thing or two about unraveling mysteries along the way.

Kat and Harper had reminded Edith that she was an adventurer at heart, and she'd repaid them by using her extensive book collection to help them solve their case. When her seaside cottage became Bluebell Bay's official library, Edith named it the Armchair Adventurers' Club. When she wasn't hosting children's book clubs, she was usually researching the latest forensic techniques. She often joked that if Sergeant Singh ever checked her internet history, he'd find searches for undetectable poisons, lethal weapons, and how best to hide a body.

"One never knows what'll prove useful when the Wolfe and Lamb detective agency takes on another case," she'd tell Kat and Harper. "If you have a crime conundrum, I want to help you find a solution."

The library doubled as Edith's home and was an irresistible combination of pre-loved and new books, freshly baked cookies and cakes, and a selection of comfy reading chairs and nooks between shelves full of novels. During the school year, Kat spent most afternoons doing her homework at a table with a harbor view.

"One minute to nine," said Harper.

Edith snapped upright. "I'm on it!" She tapped at a remote, and a TV slid out from between the bookshelves. The catchy drumbeat that heralded the *Fast News* bulletin boomed into the room. Xena's skull find was the second headline: JURASSIC DRAGON TEAM UNCOVER GRISLY KEY TO MISSING-MAN MYSTERY.

"Grisly?" said Harper. *"Really?"*

"It's the go-to adjective of crime reporters," Edith informed her.

Kat leaned forward. "Shh!"

An over-tanned anchorman said solemnly, "Idyllic Bluebell Bay has long been considered one of the jewels in Britain's seaside crown: historic, pretty as a picture, and, most important, safe. That changed last Sunday when a cliff disintegrated, revealing a two-hundred-million-year-old 'dragon' dinosaur. Just four days later, a paleontology volunteer made a gruesome discovery—assisted by a celebrity dog. We're going live to Dorset, where *Fast News* reporter Rosalyn Winter has this exclusive report."

A windswept Rosalyn filled the screen. She was standing on the harbor wall, waves spitting up behind her, wearing an orange windbreaker and a grave expression.

"When Hollywood stars Ethan and Alicia Swann chose Bluebell Bay for a well-deserved vacation, they never dreamed that their beloved miniature Pomeranian would unearth a secret that had stayed buried for two years. More extraordinary still, the pocket-sized dog found the skull among the rocks and fossils being sifted through by Professor Theo Lamb and his team—the same team that discovered the dracoraptor last Sunday.

"Late last night, an extensive search by police and forensic experts turned up human remains and an I.D. card. The victim's next of kin have been notified. He has been identified as Johnny Roswell . . ."

Edith squeezed her retriever so hard that he let out a yelp. Kat looked around, but the librarian was watching the screen with rapt attention.

"Roswell was reported missing from Tooting, London, in June two years ago," Rosalyn Winter continued. "A keen amateur fossil collector, he was twenty-four at the time of his disappearance. Earlier, I asked Alicia Swann how she felt about being caught up in the drama."

The scene switched to the ocean-view suite at the Majestic. The actress was clad in funereal black from head to toe, her perfect face luminous as she gazed into the camera lens. The Pomeranian was perched on her knee, a black bow on her fluffy head.

"Xena seems so angelic," commented Harper. "You'd never know she has the temperament of a werewolf with anger-management issues."

"There are no bad dogs, only bad owners," Kat reminded her.

"But Alicia is lovely, so I don't see—"

"Shh!" said Edith.

On the screen, Alicia's eyes shone with emotion. "It's been a terrible shock, to be honest, Rosalyn. When I sent my little warrior princess to doggy day care, the last thing I expected was that she'd lead the cops to a missing person. I only hope some good will come of it and that the family of this unfortunate young man will finally get some closure. My husband and I would like to send them our condolences. We'd also like to thank Viktor, our hotel manager, for understanding that Xena needs some TLC and to be with us after the stress of last night."

"'Course she does," Rosalyn said insincerely. "The combined police forces of the U.K. failed to do in twenty-five months what Xena managed in minutes— locate Johnny Roswell. She should be given a medal by the Queen. But I'm curious, Alicia. Why did you choose Bluebell Bay for your vacation? Did you and Ethan hear about the Jurassic Dragon discovery and think, 'That would make a great movie?'"

The actress adjusted Xena's bow. "Not at all. Our trip had been planned for months. We'd heard that Bluebell Bay was a gorgeous place to get away from it all. We learned about the dinosaur only after we got here and found the town crammed. It's been a shock to realize that accidents happen even in beautiful places and to nice people. But we won't let this put us off. We're looking forward to exploring the area and maybe seeing this dragon skeleton over the next few days."

Watching Alicia's performance, Kat thought: *I don't believe you. You were lying about having a booking at the Grand Hotel Majestic.* That part of the Swanns' holiday, at least, wasn't planned. If they hadn't come for the dinosaur, what *were* they doing in Bluebell Bay with their silver sports car and out-of-this-world horse?

The couple was too good to be true; Kat felt sure of it. Xena was aggressive for a reason. Kat intended to investigate what that reason was.

Now Rosalyn Winter was interviewing Sergeant Singh. A photograph of a hollow-cheeked young man with Bambi eyes flashed up on the screen behind him.

"This tragic case highlights the dangers of the Jurassic Coast's cliffs," the policeman was saying. "I urge families and fossil hunters to keep clear of them this summer. I'd also like to appeal for witnesses. If you recognize Johnny Roswell or have any information about what he was doing in Bluebell Bay at the time of his disappearance, please contact Dorset Police HQ. There's no suspicion of foul play. All evidence points to death by misadventure."

AN INSPECTOR CALLS

"WHAT'S 'DEATH BY MISADVENTURE'?" asked Harper. She'd given in and was treating herself to an Armchair Adventurers' Club crumpet. If there was a mystery in the works, she really did need to keep up her strength.

Edith switched off the TV and poured them each a glass of lemonade. "It's when a dangerous risk is taken voluntarily. If Johnny Roswell chose to go fossil hunting on a precipice, the coroner will rule that he understood he was taking a chance but did it anyway."

Harper and Kat shifted on their beanbags, thinking guiltily about Kat's near-disastrous bid to rescue Pax.

Edith wiped away a tear. "I can't believe that lovely young man is gone."

Now she had their full attention.

"You were friends with Johnny?" Harper was aghast.

"Goodness, no. I only ever talked to him twice, but he left an indelible impression on me. I can see him now, face aglow, as he showed me an ammonite he'd found at Kimmeridge Bay. He was wearing a SAVE SHEFFIELD'S TREES T-shirt and was so skinny that whenever he turned sideways, it was as if he'd put on an invisibility cloak. He told me he was a nature writer, but it didn't seem to pay him enough to eat. He was a contented spirit though—passionate about fossil collecting and saving the environment."

Edith hugged the retriever as Toby licked another tear off her cheek. "Seems as if one of those enthusiasms cost him his life."

"Was Johnny here on holiday?" asked Kat.

"Couldn't tell you, love, but I know a man who could. Harry Holt and Johnny were inseparable for a time. I'd see them from my window, scrambling over the cliffs at all hours in search of ammonites, brittle stars, brachiopod shells, and other bits. Rain, sleet, or snow, they were out there."

Harper put down her plate. "Harry Holt? Is that the weirdo who's been protesting the dracoraptor excavation with blood-splattered signs?"

Kat jumped in eagerly. "Ollie Merriweather told us that Harry's one of those local eccentric weirdos who come out of the woodwork wherever paleontologists are working." She giggled. "We were there when Harry sprang at Ollie and ranted on about how Professor Lamb didn't understand what forces he was unleashing."

She mimicked his Dorset accent and deep voice. "'When blood is spilled, as blood will surely be, don't say Harry didn't warn you.'"

"It was hilarious." Harper giggled. "He's been out there with a placard ever since, twittering on about ancient darkness. 'Ooh, Professor, let sleeping dragons lie.'"

They stopped. Edith wasn't laughing. She was staring at them with a mixture of sadness and disappointment.

Kat clapped a hand to her mouth. "Oh, gosh— Harry's a friend of yours, isn't he?"

Harper felt unwell. "Edith, I'm so sorry. We didn't think."

"No," said Edith, "you did not. If I didn't know from personal experience how kind you're capable of being, I'd suspend you both from the library for flying to judgment on an innocent man. As detectives, you should be ashamed of yourselves. Tell me, what was it about Harry that made you regard him as an 'eccentric weirdo,' to borrow your words? Was it his wild hair and crooked teeth?"

Harper stared hard at the floor.

"How about his tattered, stained clothes? Or was it what he said about forces of darkness and blood being spilled?"

Kat squirmed. "Umm."

"Edith's right, Kat," said Harper. "We call ourselves detectives, but we didn't ask the most basic question: Why? What made Harry think Dad didn't know what he was digging up? Did he suspect foul play when Johnny disappeared two years ago? Or is he psychic? After all, blood *has* been spilled. It's old blood, but it's still blood."

"We weren't interested because we'd already put Harry into a box labeled 'Barking Mad Local,'" answered Kat, shame-faced. "Sorry, Edith."

"*Ach*, don't be too hard on yourselves. Many older and wiser detectives than you have made the same mistake. It's Harry you should apologize to, not me."

Edith got to her feet with difficulty and put on the kettle. "You asked if Harry and I were friends. Once upon a time, I suppose we were. When I was a school librarian, he was my shiest student, bullied because he was obsessed with fossils even then. I like to hope that with my influence, books became his friends. He was my best reader. And as is often the way, books helped him make real friends."

"The way they did with the three of us?" said Kat, anxious to make amends.

Edith smiled. "Exactly, love."

"What did Harry do next, when he grew up?"

"He was smart enough to go to university but was forced to quit school in his teens to take care of his sick mum. On the rare occasions I'd run into him, we'd chat about books and fossils. His depth of knowledge was phenomenal. I dare say he could teach your father a thing or two about fossils on the Jurassic Coast, Harper. After his mum died, he was very lonely, and I was glad when he found a friend in Johnny, a fellow fossil fanatic."

Her hands trembled as she spooned Darjeeling leaves into a teapot. "I have a confession. Last year, the talk around town was that Harry had quit his job at the hardware store and become a virtual hermit. I was too caught up with my own troubles to wonder why. Then last month, he came to the Armchair Adventurers' Club and asked to borrow a book. He knew what he wanted and was gone in minutes. I was helping a couple of children, so I couldn't spare long to catch up. I did inquire after Johnny and ask why I hadn't seen him in a while. I thought he might have been ill or moved away."

"What did Harry say?" asked Harper.

"It was strange, really. He said quite curtly, 'He's gone, that's all I know. If you ask me, they didn't like what he was doing, so they put a stop to it.'"

A tingle ran through Kat. "What did he mean?"

"To be frank, I thought that he and Johnny had had a falling out, and it was an excuse. Before I could respond, he was shuffling out. I thought I heard him mutter that it was all his fault, but I can't be sure. I wasn't aware that

Johnny had been missing for nearly two years at that point."

Harper gave Kat an *Are you thinking what I'm thinking?* nudge.

Edith stirred her tea with unnecessary vigor. "In case your suspicious minds put two and two together and make five, I refuse to believe Harry had anything to do with Johnny's death. He's the most meek and mild soul in town."

Kat was skeptical. The man who'd lunged, hissing, at Ollie had seemed both fearful and fanatical. There'd been nothing meek and mild about him.

Conscious she was being judgmental again, she told herself off for letting her imagination run amok. If Johnny Roswell had had an accident while "scrambling" over the cliffs in all weathers, it was hardly surprising. There was no mystery. She and Harper should put it out of their heads and enjoy the summer.

Unfortunately, her brain had other ideas. Unanswered questions kept pinging into it. If Harry and Johnny enjoyed searching for fossils together, where was Harry when the cliff gave way? Or if Johnny had been alone, *why* was he by himself? Had they fought, as Edith suspected? Or was Johnny in search of some fossil he didn't want Harry to know about? Something precious, like the dracoraptor?

Harper was also deep in thought. "Edith," she said, "what book did Harry borrow?"

"Let me think. It's on the tip of my tongue . . . He never returned it, that I can tell you. Kept it past its due date, then pushed a note though my letterbox saying he'd spilled coffee on it and left a battered copy of *The Hobbit* and some magazines as compensation."

A no-nonsense knock interrupted her. To Kat's ears, it was the demanding rap of a man working against the clock to find answers at 9:36 A.M. An official on official business.

"I knew it!" she said triumphantly when she opened the door to Sergeant Singh. "I could have told you there's been foul play."

"There certainly has," he said with disapproval. "And where is your partner in crime? Is she here?"

"What partner in crime? Do you mean Harper?"

He tucked his navy-blue helmet under one arm. "How many partners in crime do you have, Kat Wolfe?"

Unsteady footsteps tip-tapped into the hall. "Are you going to keep Bluebell Bay's best bobby on the doorstep, Kat? Join us for a cup of tea, Sergeant Singh?"

"Thanks, Edith, but I'm in a hurry. I'd like a brief word with Misses Wolfe and Lamb, if I may."

In the library, Harper climbed out of a beanbag and beamed at him. "Have you come to ask for our assistance in solving the crime, Sergeant Singh?"

"Indeed, I do need your assistance solving the crime."

"You do?" Kat was wary. More often than not, an amused glint in the sergeant's eyes betrayed the sense of humor that lay beneath his formal manner. That morning, it was absent. Purple quarter moons of sleeplessness and crossness tugged them downward.

He took out his notebook. "I have it on good authority that a girl matching your description, Kat Wolfe, was observed taking life-threatening risks on the cliff steps last Saturday at around four thirty in the afternoon, minutes before the cliff collapsed."

Kat's heart began to pound. "I wasn't . . . I didn't . . ."

He glowered at Harper. "And I have it from two different sources that a girl matching your description, Harper Lamb, was seen on the deck of Avalon Heights—a house that has been locked and empty for months—the same afternoon. I should caution you that any girl, or girls, found to have done such a thing could be charged with breaking and entering."

"Sergeant Singh, I must object to these outrageous accusations," chastised Edith. "My dedicated young library assistants would never mess about on cliffs or 'break and enter' so much as a bar of chocolate."

"Thanks, Edith, but it *was* me on the cliff steps," said Kat, knowing that denial was pointless. "Only, I wasn't taking risks for fun. I was saving a life."

"What life?" Sergeant Singh asked disbelievingly.

"A dog's life. Harper and I found a wounded stray—a border collie. We took her to the animal clinic, and Mum stitched her up."

The policeman turned on Harper. "And what's your excuse, young lady? How do you explain your presence on the deck of a locked house? Let me guess. You were rescuing a lost kitten?"

"You're asking the wrong question," Harper said smoothly.

"Am I now?" Sergeant Singh started to simmer. "And what, in your opinion, is the right question?"

"You should be asking if we witnessed anything unusual."

Kat saw where she was going and seized the chance to turn the interview around. She and Harper had discussed the possibility that the cliff was blown up on purpose, but the discovery of the Jurassic Dragon had pushed it to the backs of their minds.

Now she said, "What Harper means, Sergeant Singh, is that if you've finally figured out that the cliff didn't come crashing down all by itself, you might want to check if we noticed anything."

The policeman did an excellent impression of a haddock out of water. "How could you possibly . . . ? Where did you hear . . . ? I didn't say . . ."

"For goodness' sake, spit it out, Sergeant," Edith said

impatiently. "Why don't you ask the girls what they saw and stop fussing about trivial concerns?"

"Breaking and entering is not a trivial concern!"

"If you vow not to get us into trouble, we'll tell you what we know," Harper bargained.

He was incredulous. "You're blackmailing a policeman?"

"Nonsense, Sergeant," scolded Edith. "It's only reasonable that the girls' memories will improve if you promise not to punish them for nobly rescuing a dog. Is that about the size of it, Kat and Harper?"

Kat grinned. "Pretty much."

Sergeant Singh groaned. "Three against one doesn't seem fair. I'm not making any promises, girls, but if the dog story is true, I'll consider overlooking your other offenses. Once more, with feeling, did you spot anything out of the ordinary before the cliff fell?"

"A ginormous shark!" announced Harper.

"The collie saw it too," Kat informed him. "She barked herself hoarse."

He glared at them. "Is this a joke?"

"No joke," said Kat. "I also saw an orange flare, like a sailor's distress signal. Seconds after that, the cliff shook as if a bomb had gone off underground."

Sergeant Singh tugged at the shadow on his chin. "Interesting. That fits with what we found yesterday— evidence that two explosions were triggered remotely."

Harper said excitedly, "That would explain the vibrations we felt at . . ." She clammed up. She'd almost admitted to being in the house.

"What kind of madman would want to endanger lives or destroy Bluebell Bay's historic cliffs?" demanded Edith.

"You'd be surprised." Sergeant Singh jotted down notes. "Vandals, teenage arsonists, rabbit hunters, fossil collectors, or even a shop or hotel owner hoping to get rich fast. A lot of folks have made a lot of money over the past week."

"I don't understand why any of that matters when you have a dead body on your hands," said Kat. "What if Johnny Roswell's death wasn't an accident? What if someone was out to get him?"

Sergeant Singh put away his notebook. "Correctly speaking, it wasn't a body; it was a skeleton. And what sort of killer do you have in mind? A fellow ammonite collector? They're ten a penny around here, you know—both ammonites and collectors. Or were you thinking that a rival nature writer, jealous of Johnny's articles on 'How to Build a Hedgehog Superhighway' or 'Top Tips for Making Compost,' pushed him under a falling boulder?"

The library phone rang. Edith reached for it but not before sending a reproachful glance the policeman's way.

He said more kindly, "Kat, I haven't forgotten how

helpful you were on that other business earlier this year. And, Harper, I realize you're somewhat traumatized after finding the skull yesterday. Let me give you both some advice. Don't go looking for mysteries where none exist. As Mrs. Swann said on the news this morning, accidents happen, even in beautiful places and to nice people."

"It's from a movie," said Harper.

"Eh?"

"That line—it's from one of Alicia's movies: *Apple Pie and Lies.*"

Edith came over with the phone. "Sergeant Singh, it's for you."

"Apologies, Edith—my phone's battery died, and I told the station I'd be here." He moved away to the window. "Yes, Constable Tibs. Can't it wait? . . . I see . . . *No!* . . . You're sure? . . . I'm leaving now. Be there ASAP."

He hung up, looking dazed. "Seems I was gravely mistaken. There's more to Johnny Roswell's death than meets the eye. Harry Holt just walked into the police station and confessed to murder."

ADVENTURES IN CYBERSPACE

IT WAS PECULIARLY UNSATISFYING SOLV-
ing a mystery in the space of a few hours.

"You look like the cats that didn't get the cream,"
teased Nettie, setting a tray of Tuscan bean soup
and warm sourdough rolls on the table shared by the
oviraptor at Paradise House. Breakfast seemed like a long
time ago, and the girls were hungry again. "Bottomless
pits," Nettie often called them. Sipping soup beneath
the dinosaur's rib cage, Kat half expected it to roar to
life and make a meal of her as she ate her own.

"Why so gloomy, Harper?" the housekeeper persisted.
"It's the school holidays, the sun's shining, and the beach
is open again if you fancy a swim. Or are you still jit-
tery after that actress's dog found the skull among the
fossils? Can't say I blame you. It's a bad business. No

wonder your dad's banned you from visiting the old hall for a while.

"Still, I'm sure you'll be as relieved as I am to hear there's been an arrest. Margo at the deli told me that a local man turned himself in this morning. Sergeant Singh must be pleased to have wrapped up the case so quickly. An unsolved murder would certainly have taken the shine off Bluebell Bay's wholesome image."

If she was expecting them to react with shock and awe, she was disappointed. They murmured politely, then went on eating their soup. As the door swung shut behind Nettie, Harper pushed away her bowl.

"Nettie's right, you know. We should be happy because the sun's out, the case is closed, and we were one step ahead of the police yet again. So why do I feel as flat as a soda with no fizz?"

Kat was equally downcast. "Last night, when I thought we had a new mystery on our hands, it was so thrilling. I could see leads going off in every direction. Now it's over. This must be how Sherlock Holmes felt when weeks went by at 221b Baker Street without a single visitor asking him to trace their missing ruby necklace or solve a locked-room murder mystery. How can we call ourselves detectives if nobody ever needs our help?"

Harper picked pumpkin seeds off her roll and fed them to the parrot perched on her shoulder. "Funny, when Edith was trying to convince us that Harry Holt was a saint, I was a hundred percent certain he was a murderer. But ever since he confessed to being a killer, all I can think is, what if he's not?"

"It feels wrong," agreed Kat. "It's too easy. I keep going over what he said to Edith when she wanted to know why Johnny hadn't been around: *If you ask me, they didn't like what he was doing, so they put a stop to it.* Who are *they*? What was Johnny doing that *they* didn't like? And what if *they* put a stop to him—permanently?"

Harper lit up like a Christmas tree at the prospect of a new line of inquiry. "The first rule of being a detective is to *question everything*. So let's do that. Why would Harry confess to a murder he didn't commit? Doesn't make sense."

"Three reasons," said Kat, ticking them off on her fingers. "One, he's afraid of something or someone. Two, he's an attention seeker and/or mentally ill. Three, he didn't do it but feels guilty about Johnny's death, maybe because he encouraged him to go fossil hunting on an unstable cliff."

"If any of those things are true, we have ourselves a case," declared Harper. "If Harry *did* cause his friend's death, let's find out why he did it and give Sergeant Singh extra evidence. If he's innocent, let's save him."

When Nettie came in to clear away their empty bowls, she found the girls transformed. They were bouncing around the living room, smiling mysteriously.

She chalked it up to the soup, a secret recipe passed down by her Welsh grandmother.

Bailey had returned to his preferred spot on the dinosaur's head. He was parroting a line from *The Big Sleep*, a detective film he'd watched at least ten times.

"'I'm getting cuter every minute,'" he cackled, and burped up a pumpkin seed.

The girls met at Harper's house the next day.

"We need to work out who Harry meant when he said *they* didn't like what Johnny was doing," suggested Kat. "Was he talking about Johnny's bosses from one of the nature magazines he wrote for, or did he mean rival fossil hunters? Or was it something personal? Maybe Johnny had fallen in with a bad crowd in London. If we can find them, we'll find the key that unlocks the whole mystery."

"Hmm," murmured Harper, her fingers flashing across the keyboard of her laptop.

In the real world, Harper often felt inescapably earthbound. Even before her accident, she'd never been athletic. Breaking both legs falling off Charming Outlaw meant that horse riding, the one physical activity for which she did have some talent, was off the menu. Though she wouldn't admit it, she'd lost her nerve.

All of that was forgotten when she sat down at a computer. She'd been a toddler when her Cuban American archaeologist mother had passed away, but

Carmen's genius for languages and advanced mathematics lived on in her daughter. Online, Harper felt free. Coding lent her wings. Whenever she embarked on a hacking mission, it amused her to imagine her laptop's keyboard as the controls of a fighter jet. She'd mentally don a flight jacket, goggles, and a scarf (like Amelia Earhart) and salute her wingman (Bailey) before taking off.

Today, she confined herself to a gulp of ginger beer. After all, Google searches were something a toddler could do.

She began with the basics. Who was Johnny Roswell and what did he do?

It wasn't hard. He'd been both a journalist and a missing person. She had scores of results in seconds.

Johnny had begun his career as a blogger and was soon writing for gardening and nature magazines. Though his early articles showed a distinct lack of promise, he'd improved rapidly. Shortly before he disappeared, he'd won a Wildlife Champion Award for his story "In Defense of Urban Foxes."

"What a good person he was," said Kat as Harper clicked on one caring article after another: "How to Attract Bees to Your Garden!" "Twenty-Five Ways to Ditch Plastic!" "How to Save Orphaned Baby Birds!"

"Yeah, it's hard to believe anyone would feel

murderous after reading any of these," remarked Harper. "Kinda the opposite."

"How about fossil collecting? Did he ever write about that? Maybe he was murdered for something rare or valuable."

Harper did find a blog by Johnny on a fossil website, but it gave no hint of any special find. It was about collecting responsibly, without harming birds or plants. Fossils were Johnny's hobby, but it seemed he loved helping the environment above all else. He was fond of quoting a Native American proverb: "When the last tree is cut down, the last fish eaten, and the last stream poisoned, you will realize that you cannot eat money."

Kat noticed the time. "Sorry, Harper—I have to fly. I promised Alicia I'd take Xena for a walk this afternoon."

With Kat gone, Harper turned to the missing-person reports. She soon saw why Johnny Roswell's disappearance had caused so few ripples. A typed note had been found in his apartment telling friends and family he planned to end it all.

The only person who didn't believe he'd taken his own life was his sister, Joanne, a marine biologist in Florida. After he vanished, she told *The Guardian* she was positive her brother's death was suspicious because his laptop had vanished with him, but that the police refused to believe her.

"I know Johnny didn't write that note because he addressed me as Joanne, which he never did in real life. He always called me by my childhood nickname, JoJo, or sometimes J.K., a reference to Harry Potter author J. K. Rowling. We were big fans of her books when we were younger."

Harper continued reading:

"Johnny was too fired up about changing the world to ever think about ending his life. A week before he went missing, he told me that he was working on a story—an "exposé"—that was going to be huge. He was bubbling over with excitement. He said, 'When I'm done, JoJo, everyone will see these monsters for who they really are.' The way he said it sent a shiver through me. I was late for a meeting, so I wished him luck and said goodbye. It was the last time we ever spoke. I'd give anything to be able to go back in time and ask, '*which* monsters?' Who did he mean?"

Chilled, Harper shut down the page. An exposé was when a reporter uncovered something embarrassing or damaging. Had Johnny been on the verge of revealing the truth about an environment-destroying company?

Could it be the weed-killer manufacturer he'd warned readers about in his piece on organic vegetables?

Nettie wandered in, smiling and chatty. "What are you up to, Harper?"

Harper tapped a key, and a Latin tutorial boomed into the room. Few things guaranteed peace like a Latin lesson. "*Amor vincit omnia*," she intoned. "Love conquers all."

Five seconds later, Nettie remembered something was burning on the stove.

Alone again, Harper dialed the Grand Hotel Majestic's restaurant. It was the first chance she'd had to attempt to discover who Ollie Merriweather had met for lunch the previous Wednesday. She'd come up with what she thought was an excellent story about how her boss, Oliver Merriweather, needed to write a thank-you card to the business associate he'd dined with but couldn't remember his last name. Was it on the reservation?

The receptionist was friendly but unhelpful. Regrettably, she was unable to give out any details unless Mr. Merriweather contacted the reservations team himself.

Professor Lamb was due home at any moment. With no time to lose, Harper returned to her laptop, put on her imaginary aviator outfit, saluted Bailey, and used a few simple coding tricks to slip like a wraith through the firewall of the Grand Hotel Majestic.

Harper had been taught how to hack and stay safe by a former student of Professor Lamb's. She was an apprentice with only a fraction of Jasper's skills, but she was catching up fast. Getting past the Majestic's flimsy security system was child's play for her. Soon she was whizzing around the hotel's internal reservation system as nimbly as any staff member.

The lunch had been booked in Ollie's name, leaving her none the wiser about his companion. She did find the bill, which came to a staggering £199.76 for two people and included lobster and champagne. Harper doubted that Oliver Merriweather's student loan would have covered it. She'd need to investigate him further.

It was eye-opening, getting an insight into life behind the scenes at the Majestic. No wonder Viktor Karlsson was stressed. Naughty guests stole bathrobes, broke lamps and coffee machines, and spilled red wine on cream carpets and then denied it. Naughty staff quit without warning, bickered incessantly, stole fillet steaks, and were forever destroying guests' expensive belongings.

Out of curiosity, Harper looked up the Swanns' booking. As she and Kat had suspected, Viktor had given them another couple's room. It didn't prove that the actors had lied about having a reservation, though. If their travel agent had messed up, it might have been a genuine error.

Clicking on the ocean-view suite brought up a

chain of emails between Viktor and the Swanns, most of which were complaints about Xena. The Pomeranian had peed on a rug, chewed a cushion, kept fellow guests awake yapping until the small hours, and attacked the chambermaids. Viktor was having to pay them triple-time wages to clean their room.

To each imploring message, Alicia sent an identical reply.

Sorry, lovely Viktor! Thanks for your
understanding. Happy to pay for any damage! XX

Her last email must have been sent to the hotel in error. It appeared to be an unfinished draft, meant for someone who wasn't the manager of the Grand Hotel Majestic.

Darling,
You're panicking about nothing. What is KW
going to do? She's just a . . .

Harper's breath caught in her throat. She had the feeling that she was looking at something important. Sinister, even. Millions of people had the same initials as Kat Wolfe. There was a 99.9 percent probability that Alicia was talking about someone else. But what if she wasn't?

She's just a . . . what? Just a girl? Just a pet sitter? And who was Alicia writing to? Ethan? Her agent? A friend? A secret admirer?

Harper had been a fan of Alicia's for years and was delirious with joy that her idol had chosen Bluebell Bay for her vacation. But the email put a whole new slant on things. If it *did* happen to be about Kat, then the couple had a secret. Perhaps Alicia was ill-treating her dog and was concerned that Kat would find out.

Harper shut her laptop. She'd need to do some poking around online to see what she could uncover about the Swanns. If they'd ever had so much as an unpaid parking ticket, Harper would dig it up.

She'd do anything on earth to protect her best friend. Anything at all.

SPELLBOUND

AS THE DAUGHTER OF A STRUGGLING VET,
Kat was unaccustomed to VIP treatment, and after
the manager of the Majestic hailed her arrival with the
fawning reverence he generally reserved for film stars
and billionaires, she decided she didn't care for it.

"Kat Wolfe, it is our pleasure to welcome you once
more to the Grand Hotel Majestic! Are you here to
collect Mrs. Swann's unique Pomeranian? I'll dial her
suite. While you wait, allow me to order you a drink on
the house. I can recommend our famed salted caramel
milkshake. When you're ready, Belinda, our customer
services manager, will escort you to the ocean-view
suite."

But when the elevator halted at the third floor and
Kat stepped into the hallway, Belinda remembered that
she had an important appointment elsewhere. "You can't

go wrong," she told Kat, stabbing repeatedly at the lobby button. "The ocean-view suite is the last door on the right." Still speaking, she was sucked away into the bowels of the building.

Kat was on her own.

The corridor was bathed in a vanilla glow. As she summoned the courage to march to the end, the door nearest her crashed open. A man with fleshy features and hairy arms nearly bowled her over. He didn't apologize.

"I think you dropped something," said Kat, noticing a gold glint on the carpet behind him.

His lip curled. "Is not mine. Give to me. I take to reception."

Kat got to it before he did. "Thanks, but it might belong to my client. I'll check with her first."

She picked up what looked like a credit card and walked on slowly, pausing to study it after the elevator had taken the rude man away. It was a black metal card embossed with a gold dragon, its tail twisted into an infinity symbol. She flipped it over, but there were no identifying numbers, names, or signatures on it.

Conscious that she was already late, she tucked it into the back pocket of her jeans and continued to the ocean-view suite. Inside, Alicia was scolding someone.

"It's no good looking at me with those angel eyes. Mommy's mad at you. What am I going to say to Daddy? Those are his favorite crocodile-hide boots from Italy."

Kat rang the bell. Alicia greeted her with a theatrical eye roll. "Hey there, Kat Wolfe. Good thing you're here to whisk my warrior princess away. She feels smothered by the endless rules and regs in this stuffy hotel. She's been acting up."

Alicia smiled as Xena leaped into Kat's arms and nearly licked her to death. "Look what those needle teeth did to Ethan's best boots."

Privately, Kat thought Xena had done Ethan a gigantic favor. The boots were hideous. She'd put the Pom down and was sympathizing about the chewed leather out of politeness when she noticed Alicia's leopard-print tote bag on the table. When she'd first seen it, she'd assumed it was fake fur. But something about the silky, subtle sheen of it made her wonder if it was real. Surely no one with one ounce of decency would consider buying a bag made from an actual leopard. She must be mistaken, she reassured herself.

Before she could think about it further, Xena began yapping and clawing at the closed bathroom door. Alicia paid no attention.

"I'd better order another pair of boots before Ethan notices they're missing and all hell breaks loose," she confided. Handing Kat a leash patterned with faux diamonds, she dismissed her with a bright "Okay, kids—have fun."

As Kat pried Xena away from the bathroom door, a

strong herbal scent wafted out. Bubble bath? A scented candle? She clutched the wriggling Pom to her chest. "I'll bring Xena back in an hour, Mrs. Swann."

"Darling, you must have her for longer than that! Take her to the beach. Enjoy! Keep her overnight if you fancy it! Grumpy Viktor would be thrilled."

Kat knew that wouldn't work because she still had Mr. Bojangles to visit and Pax to walk when she got home, but before she could protest, the actress turned a radiant gaze on her.

"Kat Wolfe, this gift you have of communicating with animals, it's awesome. I'm lost in admiration. Ethan thinks you're a wizard with horses too. Thanks for taking us on."

Kat melted and found herself unable to mention Pax or Mr. B, or the fact that neither she nor the Lambs had so far been paid for livery, horse feed, grooming, or dog sitting. She also forgot to ask about the gold-and-black card.

"You're welcome," she mumbled, stricken with shyness.

Leaving the hotel with Xena, Kat's head felt fuzzy. She kept seeing Alicia's serene, knowing smile as she praised her. It was the same one the actress had used on Viktor when he couldn't find her booking.

It was, Kat thought later, as if she'd been hypnotized.

ESCAPE ARTISTS

THE SPELL ALICIA HAD CAST OVER HER was still working an hour later as Kat hesitated outside Mario Rossi's motor home, clutching Xena's leash in one hand and her phone in the other. She'd written five different versions of a text explaining that Pomeranians and pythons didn't mix, and it would be best for everyone if she could return Xena to the Grand Hotel Majestic right away. Once again, she deleted it.

She tied the dog's leash to an iron rung. "Sit, Xena. Stay," she instructed. "I won't be long."

The miniature Pom lay down obediently and rested her nose on her sandy paws. She was worn out. Bluebell Bay was one of the few local beaches to allow dogs in the summer, and Xena had swum and chased balls with two manic Jack Russells. While she was playing, Kat had spotted the harbormaster picking up plastic litter. She'd asked him if there'd been any shark sightings around the time the cliff fell the previous Saturday.

"*Sharks?* This isn't Martha's Vineyard, you know, home of the hungry great white. There are a few fierce crabs and minnows I could show you, but otherwise I promise it's quite safe to get back in the water." His laughter had followed her as she sprinted off to catch Xena, who'd stolen a child's ice cream.

Letting herself into Mario's space-age motor home a short while later, Kat wondered again what he did for a living. There was a new photo of him in a frame on the coffee table. His black hair was wet, and he was grinning in a helmet, balanced on an upturned camouflage kayak.

Because Kat was a detective to her fingertips, she couldn't resist inspecting the cupboard where she'd seen the squeaky-clean coasteering equipment the day before. The helmet, wet suit, and buoyancy aid were still there, but now looked as if they'd been used. Mario had told the truth about that.

In the bedroom, she heaved a sigh. The vivarium lid was hanging off. Mr. B had escaped again.

She was about to search for him when she noticed a pungent herbal scent similar to the one in the Swanns' suite. It reminded her of an excellent Chinese liniment her mum and Nurse Tina used if an animal had muscular aches and pains. She sourced it to the black lacquered cabinet.

The top drawer was locked, but the other, larger drawer rolled open, clinking as it did so. With the exception of a bag of shitake mushrooms, it was packed with glass jars filled with amber or dark liquids, some of which included berries and slices of ginger. Chinese traditional medicine. All except two of the labels were in Chinese characters. There was a "Migraine Relief" salve and a yellow bottle labeled "Propolis for Wounds," both bought in Chinatown, London.

Kat considered the selection. Had Alicia been using herbal remedies such as these? Did she or Ethan get migraines or need wound treatment for Xena's bites?

A strangled yap distracted her. She ran into the living area. The door had swung open. What if the python had gotten out and was now slithering around the caravan park?

But that potential disaster paled into insignificance when she spotted a diamond lead lying twisted on the ground. Xena was missing.

Slamming the door behind her, Kat began a frenzied search. "Boy, do you have a gift with animals, Kat Wolfe," she berated herself as she tore up and down the rows of motor homes and caravans. "A gift for losing them, anyway."

She hunted the length and breadth of the caravan park. No one had seen a Pomeranian. Xena was either lost or had been snatched by dog thieves. Pomeranians—especially those owned by Hollywood stars—were in high demand. It was all Kat's fault. How would she ever be able to face Alicia Swann?

Numb with despair, she returned to the motor home. For all she knew, Mr. B was on the loose too, ready to unleash a wave of terror among the Durdle Door campers.

When she discovered him coiled up in the motor home's driver's seat, tail over the steering wheel as if he'd been planning a quick getaway, Kat could have wept with relief. "Mr. B, you can't keep doing this Houdini routine. My heart can't take it."

The python uncoiled lazily and slid between the seats, where he became wedged and could go no farther. When Kat leaned over to try to help, the cause of the obstruction became grimly apparent. His belly bulged with a Pomeranian-sized lump. Two stumpy legs were outlined, as if Xena had made a last bid for freedom before succumbing to the inevitable.

Keep Mr. B away from anything small and furry, Mario had warned.

Kat sat on the sofa, too shocked to cry. How could she have been so moronic? She'd gone hurtling around the caravan park without pausing to consider that a small scared dog was much more likely to follow her pet sitter into the motor home than go looking for trouble in the big wide world. While Kat was outside conducting a fruitless search, Xena was inside being swallowed whole.

How was she going to admit to Alicia Swann that her warrior princess had ended her days as a canapé for a royal python?

And how could she tell Mario Rossi that the reason Mr. B had indigestion was because he'd dined on a film star's Pomeranian? The fur alone would give the snake cramps.

It was the worst day of Kat's life, no competition. Her heart ached for dear little Xena. She hadn't deserved such a grisly end.

Someone rapped smartly on the door. Kat's first instinct was to hide in a cupboard. She wasn't ready to deal with Mario. Then she realized that he'd hardly knock when he had a key.

She peered through the one-way glass. A harried-looking woman gripping a pram and the hand of a ponytailed young girl glared up at the motor home.

Kat pointed a warning finger at Mr. B, still stuck between the seats: "Don't move a muscle." She opened the door a smidgeon. "Sorry, Mario's not here at the moment."

The woman said abruptly, "Do you own a Pomeranian?"

Kat gulped. Had this person witnessed Xena's gruesome demise? Was she an animal control officer? Was the video already up on YouTube, alongside the ones of anacondas swallowing alligators and cows?

Kat stepped outside, smiling sweetly. "What kind of Pomeranian?" she stalled.

"The miniature kind." The mum gestured at the stroller. "Show her, Imogen."

Grudgingly, the girl lifted the cover. Beneath it, Xena was tucked up in a Peter Rabbit blanket, her head on a baby pillow. She was fast asleep.

Kat was speechless. If this was Xena, who or what had Mr. B eaten? "Uh, yes, that's my Pom. Thanks for bringing her back."

"I can't apologize enough," said the mum. "Immie's been begging me for a dog since she was old enough to talk. She saw yours and couldn't resist playing with her. I don't know what came over her. You must have been so worried." She let out a sigh. "It was only a game," she went on defensively. "She wasn't stealing her, I promise. Say sorry, Immie."

Kat's heart went out to the girl. "It's okay, Immie, really it is. I adore dogs as much as you do, so I understand. Xena can be nervous of strangers though. Did she try to nip you or growl at you?"

The ponytail shook. "No, she loved me. She was gentle."

Kat studied her thoughtfully. "Immie, would you mind looking after Xena for a few more minutes?" she asked as she put the leash on Xena and lifted her out of the stroller. "There's something I need to do."

"She'd love to," said the grateful mum. "We're in that caravan over there."

Back in the motor home, Kat found the note Mario had left in plain view on the kitchen counter. Had she seen it earlier, it would have saved her forty minutes of suffering.

Hi, Kat,
You'll notice that Mr. B has gained a few kgs overnight! He's been off his food for weeks but decided this a.m. to devour a chicken I'd left defrosting on the counter. No dinner for me! Thanks for taking care of him.

Mario

Kat yawned. It had been a big day. The Armchair Adventurers' Club breakfast with Edith and Harper and getting the surprising news about Harry Holt felt as if they had happened a week ago, not a mere eight hours earlier. It was strange to think that Harry was in a cell, and Wolfe & Lamb had a new mission: clear his name or help prove beyond a doubt that he killed Johnny Roswell.

With the chicken in his tummy, Mr. B weighed twice as much as usual. It took all of Kat's strength and python-whispering skills to ease him out from between the seats and lug him over to the vivarium. He was sleepy and looked extremely sorry for himself. Indigestion is no fun for anyone, not even royal snakes.

Before Kat left, she petted him and apologized for wrongly accusing him of gobbling Xena. She didn't care what anyone said—pythons have feelings too.

HAMILTON PARK

THE BENTLEY WAS PEARLY GREEN AND glistened like a forest in winter. The neighbors came out to marvel at it as a suited-and-booted chauffeur stowed the Wolfes' scruffy overnight bags. Kat slid into the back seat between her mum and Harper.

"It's a miracle! I can't believe we're finally on our way to Hamilton Park."

The chauffeur put the key in the ignition. He smiled at Kat's mum in the rearview mirror. "If everyone is comfortable, shall we be on our way, Dr. Wolfe?"

"Yes, thanks! No, wait!" said the vet all in one breath as her phone rang in her handbag.

"Don't answer it," begged Kat, to no avail.

"Oh no!" said Dr. Wolfe. "What a disaster. Hold on a moment, I'm going to try to get a better signal." She climbed out of the car.

Kat hopped out too, chest tight with disappointment. "What's the beastly prime minister forcing Grandfather to do this time?" she demanded when her mum got off the phone. "What excuse does the PM have today?"

"Watch your manners, Katarina!" Her mum cast an apologetic glance at the chauffeur. He was programming the GPS, trying not to smile.

She steered Kat away. "Honey, Janey Nowak's cat has been hit by a car and needs an emergency operation. If he survives, he'll need intensive care. How would you and Harper feel about going to Hamilton Park without me? You'll be very well looked after. I'm so sorry, but it can't be helped."

"Why do people have to drive so fast?" cried Kat. "I hope Janey's cat makes it. Don't worry, Mum—I understand."

And she did. She was proud that she had a mum who'd choose saving an animal over a luxury weekend at a stately home every time. Though it didn't stop Kat from wishing that fate hadn't intervened and that that same mum could be with her, especially when she was a nervous wreck about being reunited with her absentee grandfather.

"How about taking Pax along for the ride?" suggested her mother, reading her mind. "She can keep an eye on you for me."

Kat looked at the fine leather seats in the Bentley. "Grandfather might not want a dog in his expensive car."

They consulted the chauffeur. "If his granddaughter wishes to take her dog, I shouldn't think His Lordship would mind. He's mad about animals himself."

Kat didn't correct him on the "her dog" part. She liked the sound of it.

Shortly afterward, the Bentley climbed the narrow road out of Bluebell Bay. Kat cracked open a window and Pax put her nose to it, chocolate ears flapping in the breeze. The sun made diamonds of the sheep in the emerald fields of Dorset.

Harper gave Kat a *Look at us, off on an adventure in a Bentley!* grin, because she knew her friend was miserable about her mum not coming and nervous about staying with the grandfather she barely knew.

Kat grinned back, laughing when Pax offered her a bandaged paw. The chauffeur laughed too and invited them to help themselves to ginger beer and homemade banana bread from a hamper. Soon, it really did feel as if they were embarking on an adventure holiday.

"Thanks for coming, Harper," Kat said. "I wasn't sure if your dad could spare you."

"Honestly? I think he's thrilled that I'll be away from the Jurassic Dragon insanity for a few days. Ever since the news broke about Johnny's skull, Dad's had reporters crawling everywhere. He's had to take on extra security. It's costing a fortune."

Harper's phone peeped. It was a text from Edith, wishing them a wonderful weekend.

P.S. The book that Harry borrowed and never returned was *The Sixth Extinction*. He always was fascinated by what caused the dinosaurs to perish and whether it could happen again. BTW, he's been denied bail. A flight risk, the judge said.

A cement truck clattered by. Harper took advantage of the racket to say in Kat's ear, "If Harry's guilty, I guess the judge did the right thing. If he's innocent, we need to prove it as fast as we can."

"We'll carry on investigating while we're at Hamilton Park," her friend reassured her.

"*How?* Dad insisted I leave my laptop behind. Apparently, I could use more fresh air."

"We'll find a way."

The journey to Buckinghamshire's Chiltern Hills took two and a half hours. While Harper slept, Kat watched the scenery go by, wondering whether Mr. B had recovered from his tummy ache and whether Orkaan and Outlaw were behaving for Nettie. Kat hoped Tina was coping with Xena. She'd persuaded the veterinary nurse to take care of the Pomeranian for the weekend after Alicia had texted late on Friday to say that she'd come down with a cold and Ethan was running a fever.

NATURALLY, we don't want to pass on our germs. Any chance you can take care of my WARRIOR PRINCESS till Monday?? WE'LL PAY YOU DOUBLE!! Thanks, Kat Wolfe! GREATEST pet sitter EVER! A.S.

Alicia had been as fit as an Olympian when Kat saw her just five hours earlier, so it was hard to credit that the actress was suddenly at death's door, as she'd claimed. However, clouds of herbal steam *had* been issuing from her bathroom, so it was just possible that she'd been inhaling eucalyptus or tea tree oil to ease her sinuses.

No problem! Get well soon! Kat had texted back, even though finding an eleventh-hour pet sitter for a dog with Xena's personality problems was a big problem. Had Tina not come to the rescue, she'd have been stuck.

Now, she debated whether to text Alicia to check whether she or Ethan had dropped the black metal card with the gold dragon on it. In the end, she decided against it. If the card did belong to the Swanns, they might insist that the chauffeur turn the Bentley around and drive to the Grand Hotel Majestic that very minute. As far as Kat was concerned, they could jolly well wait till Monday. She was going to Hamilton Park if it was the last thing she did.

She dozed after that, surfacing as the Bentley braked in front of fortified iron gates flanked by snarling concrete lions and a bank of CCTV cameras. An armed guard with a clipboard bent down to inspect the girls and dog. Then they proceeded along an avenue of five-hundred-year-old oaks with roots like dinosaur feet. Branches entwined overhead.

Pax whimpered and pressed her nose to the window. A dark bay horse was flying across a meadow. A wiry rider with short spiky hair bent low over its shoulders. As Kat watched, a pheasant exploded from the long grass in their path. The horse shied so violently it almost fell.

The ancient trunks of the oaks interrupted Kat's view. She held her breath, certain that the rider must be lying smashed to pieces. But when the pair reappeared, the rider was on board and the horse was cantering easily. They sailed over a five-barred gate and were gone.

Awed, Kat said, "Who *was* that?"

"Who was who?" asked the chauffeur.

Harper sat up. "What did I miss?"

"The best rider I've ever seen. A teenage boy, I think. His horse was spooked by a pheasant."

The driver braked to avoid a squirrel. "That would be a guest. We get a lot of them. Get a lot of wildlife at Hamilton Park too. His Lordship won't allow any shooting on the estate." He chuckled. "Sometimes I think he prefers animals to people."

Kat felt better. If her grandfather loved animals as much as she did, they'd get along fine.

"He's a good man," the chauffeur went on, "but you'd never know it from the newspapers. They call him the Dark Lord, and not just because his first name is Dirk. He is tough, I grant you that. Wouldn't be minister of defense if he wasn't. But around the estate, you won't hear naught said against him."

Lord Hamilton-Crosse's house was on the brow of a forested hill. As the Bentley crunched to a halt in the gravel of the circular drive, Kat felt an overpowering urge to scream at the chauffeur to drive on. She wanted to go home to her mum and the animal clinic, where everything was normal and didn't reek of money.

There was nothing regular about Hamilton Park. Not the paddocks of gleaming horses or fields of pedigreed goats and cows. Not the landscaped gardens of roses and lavender. Not the maze. And certainly not the seventeenth-century Jacobean house, which, the chauffeur told them, had forty-eight bedrooms.

"Wonder if any are haunted," muttered Harper, and Kat giggled.

A butler opened their car door and the girls got out as a woman with elegant curls and a face creased with smile lines stepped forward to shake their hands.

"Welcome, Harper. Kat, I'm delighted to finally meet you. I'm Freya, His Lordship's personal assistant. I'm so sorry that your mum wasn't able to join us. She let me know that she was dealing with an emergency. We've had a last-minute hitch on our end too. Kat, your grandfather has been so looking forward to your visit and is devastated that he couldn't be here to greet you. Regrettably, he's been unavoidably detained."

Kat was so upset, she didn't trust herself to speak. She doubted that her grandfather knew what it meant to be devastated. If he did, he'd understand why she felt that he let her down every time she'd allowed herself to care.

"And who is this?" Freya was asking as Pax lolloped past her on three legs to meet another border collie, this one arthritic and graying at the whiskers. There was a friendly growl from Pax, and a great deal of tail wagging from the other dog, then the pair careered off through the gardens.

"Pax!" yelled Kat.

"Let them have fun," said Freya with a smile. "Flush—he's your grandfather's dog—will take good care of Pax, and so will James, our head groom. He's wild about dogs. Come this way, girls. Let me show you to your rooms."

They followed the PA into an echoing marble hallway with angels and chariots on the ceiling and a chandelier so big, it could have illuminated London. At the top of a staircase carpeted in crimson was a gallery to rival many art museums.

"Are those your ancestors?" whispered Harper as she craned her neck to look up at yet another gilded painting of unsmiling men whipping frightened horses after foxhunting dogs.

"Hope not." Kat scowled, still fuming about her grandfather's disappearing act.

Freya explained that most of the bedrooms and suites in the house were reserved for government officials and visiting dignitaries and businessmen, while those in the north wing had been turned into offices. As they passed the doorway to that wing, Kat glimpsed a warren of beige rooms and clerks as unsmiling as the men in the paintings.

"You'll be staying in the south wing, His Lordship's personal residence," said Freya. "He thought you might like the tower room."

Harper was alarmed. The "tower room" conjured up images of the freezing Tower of London room where Anne Boleyn had stayed before Henry VIII chopped off her head. It would have slit windows and ravens cawing on the sill. She'd have nightmares!

The first surprise was that the south wing bore no resemblance to the rest of the manor house. Kat had expected it to be the most decadent, gold-plated, luxurious section of all. In reality, the decor was spare and tasteful.

The floorboards smelled of beeswax polish and creaked underfoot. Every worn rug told a story of Arabian or New Mexican nights. The bookcases overflowed with well-thumbed novels, and the walls were lined with animal pictures: hares, birds, and baby foxes frolicking in the snow. Even so, the rooms had a lonely air.

"His Lordship's study," Freya informed them as they passed a closed door. They climbed more stairs. "Bet you think you'll need a compass to find your way back." She laughed. "The house can be overwhelming at first. I'll give you a map."

For Harper, the tower room was love at first sight. It was round, cozy, and had wraparound vistas of the forest and rose gardens. Best of all, it featured two four-poster beds with damask canopies.

"That's yours on the right, Harper," Freya said.

There were new pajamas on the pillow, and there was a book on the code breakers of Bletchley Park and a collection of Emily Dickinson's poems on the bedside table. There was also something else—a shiny rose-gold laptop. Harper touched it reverently.

"His Lordship wasn't sure if you'd be bringing your

own," explained Freya. "He thought you might like the use of a computer while you're here."

Kat's bedside table was stacked with mystery novels and a magnificent photographic book on horses. There were pajamas on her pillow too.

None of it made her feel better. It was obvious that Freya had organized everything. Her grandfather didn't have time to be a grandfather, so he paid other people to do it. Nevertheless, she remembered her manners, as instructed by her mum. "Thanks for going to so much trouble, Freya. It's kind of you."

"Don't thank me! It was His Lordship's doing. Everything except the pajamas, that is. He'd have been hopeless choosing those. Now, I'll leave you to freshen up. Tea will be served in the orangery."

As soon as she left, Harper began bouncing on the bed. "If I'm dreaming, don't wake me up. Cute pj's, a superfast laptop, and a princess-in-a-castle four-poster. This is one enchanted room!"

"I suppose it is, if you like that sort of thing," Kat said sulkily. She stomped downstairs to find the bathroom.

"Don't judge your granddad until you've heard his excuse," Harper called after her. "There could be a national emergency. War might have broken out."

Or maybe he just can't be bothered, Kat thought angrily as she tried to recall which door hid the bathroom. She opened the cleaning cupboard, and a mop fell out. She also found the library, the laundry, and another guest room.

The last door opened into her grandfather's study. Kat couldn't resist sneaking a peek inside. A bay window overlooked the maze and a field of horses. On the far wall was a bookcase and a painting of the Dark Lord with a Clydesdale horse and Flush the border collie. A photo of his surfer son Rufus (Kat's father), a journal, and two fountain pens were the only things on his tidy desk.

Feeling guilty about invading his personal space, Kat turned to go. It was then that she saw the childish crayon drawings on the other wall. *Her* drawings. Along with her first school photo and one of her aged two, beaming with no teeth. Also framed was a painting she'd done of a horse, a prizewinning school essay with a gold star, and a collage of a family picnic in Bluebell Bay. In the center was a photo of Kat, tousled and grinning, with her grandfather. He was formal in his shirt and smart trousers, but looked as close as he ever got to happy.

"Wow," said Harper, who'd come in silently behind her. "I don't know about you, but I'd say this proves he does care."

A grin broke like sunshine across Kat's face. "Maybe he does. A bit."

She smiled all the way to the orangery.

MONSTERS

KAT COULDN'T SLEEP. HER MIND WHIRLED from the "Kat Wolfe wall" in her grandfather's study, to the Welsh mountain pony she'd met on a tour of the stables, to the candlelit vegan feast the chef had prepared just for her and Harper.

The pony thoughts reminded her of Pax, who'd bonded with Flush, and before long she was pining for the pets in Bluebell Bay: Tiny, Xena, Charming Outlaw, Orkaan, and even escape-artist Mr. B. She winced when she recalled the near catastrophe with the Pomeranian, which in turn got her thinking about the Swanns and the Jurassic Dragon. From the dinosaur, there was only one place to go: Johnny Roswell's life and mysterious death, and Harry Holt, who might or might not be guilty.

And all the time, Kat was straining her ears for the

faintest rumble that might signal the return of her grandfather. Freya had insisted he'd be home before morning.

She tossed and turned twice more before sitting up. It was 1:20 A.M. Where was he? Disappointment prickled her again. Was she really going to spend a whole weekend at Hamilton Park without ever seeing him?

The soft clunk of a car door had her tiptoeing past Harper's bed to the window. A limousine was in the driveway. Her grandfather shook the chauffeur's hand and went inside. Kat climbed back into bed. Now that he was home, she'd be able to sleep, she thought.

At 1:45 A.M., she gave up. She was thirsty. If she nipped to the kitchen for a glass of water, she'd soon nod off.

But when she got downstairs, the light was on in her grandfather's study. As she crept by, she glimpsed him through the partly open door. He was sitting at his desk with his head in his hands, looking old and broken. That was the word that came into Kat's head. *Broken*.

Without thinking, she tapped twice and went in.

Startled, he got clumsily to his feet. "Kat! What are you doing up at this hour? Is everything all right? Are you cold? Do you need another blanket or pillow? Are you hungry? Can I fetch you something to eat or drink?"

Kat couldn't help laughing. "Grandfather, you're the one who's been working late, not me. Can I get *you* something?"

His smile reached his tired eyes. "Thanks, Kat. Do

you know, I feel better already, seeing you. I'm truly sorry for not being here when you arrived, especially . . . well, especially since I haven't been in contact much—er, at all—over the last few months. If it's any consolation, I think of you every day when I walk into my study and see your pictures. Your mum used to send them to me every Christmas. They were the best presents I ever got. Still are."

"Then why have you been avoiding us?" asked Kat, taking the liberty of curling up in an armchair.

He sighed but didn't deny it. "Too many threats."

"*Threats?* Who from?"

"From *whom*," her grandfather corrected. "Too many to mention. Most people believe that spying ended with the Cold War. In truth, it's worse than ever. If there are military, business, or cybersecrets to be stolen, someone's trying to steal them. On top of that, I'm dealing with a situation. That's why I was late today."

Kat was intrigued. She'd often wondered if he'd been a spy himself. "What situation?"

"I'm afraid I can't talk about live operations. What I *can* say is that we're in a race against time. There are people in this world who want to destroy all that's beautiful and good. We have to stop them or die trying."

A chink of ice lodged in Kat's heart. When he said "we," he meant himself, she knew. *He* had to stop them or die trying.

It reminded her of Johnny Roswell's last words to his sister: *When I'm done, JoJo, everyone will see these monsters for who they really are.* Once he'd gone, JoJo had bitterly regretted not asking her brother who he'd meant.

Not wanting any future regrets, Kat asked, "Who are they, Grandfather, these monsters?"

"Monsters?" He snapped out of a dark reverie. "Who said anything about monsters? Goodness—is that the time?"

While he was speaking, Kat had noticed a pair of Pi-Craft binoculars on his desk. They were similar to the ones in the unclaimed army briefcase she'd discovered at Avalon Heights. She'd attempted to use them, but couldn't get them to focus. Her grandfather's fountain pen was identical to the pen in her briefcase too. Kat had also tried that but found it useless. It had a scratchy nib and leaked ink.

If the minister of defense used Pi-Craft products, they were neither ordinary nor defective. Kat decided to inspect her own pen again. It could be a voice recorder. "Those binoculars—are they any good?" she asked casually.

He picked them up. "These are night-vision glasses. The best there are." He polished the lenses. "They've given me an idea. Are you sleepy, young Kat?"

"No, wide awake."

"How would you like an adventure? A horse adventure?"

"*Now?* At two in the morning?"

His haunted face creased into a grin. "No time like the present."

Kat grinned back. "Yes, please!"

He opened a cupboard and removed a parcel wrapped in brown paper. It had her name on it. "Better put these on, then. Where we're going, you'll need to keep warm."

NIGHT FLIGHT

THEY TOOK A SECRET TUNNEL TO THE stable block.

"It was put in when the house was built to give the lord of the manor the best chance of escaping by horse-back in times of war or any other emergency," explained Kat's grandfather, lifting a rug in his study to reveal a trapdoor. "The only people who know of its existence are Freya, James, my head groom—and now you."

"Do you ever use it?" asked Kat as she followed him and his weaving torch under the foundation of the old house, sneezing in the musty air. Her new riding boots squeaked.

"All the time when I was a boy—and your dad was just the same. He and his friends were forever down there playing smugglers and cops. These days, my work gets in the way of most things. I wish I could visit the stable more often. Being around animals is the fastest way of banishing stress, don't you find?"

They came up beneath the wood shavings in the Clydesdale mare's stall.

"Won't the groom mind being woken in the middle of the night?" asked Kat, reaching up to stroke the mare's white blaze.

"Why do we need James's help?" Her grandfather led the horse to the mounting block. "You know how to put on a bridle, don't you?"

"Yes, but—"

"And I think I can strap a bareback pad on my own horse. Faith and I have been friends for more than eighteen years. She's a genuine gentle giant. I'll take the reins, and you can cling on behind. If you've never been on a Clydesdale, don't be nervous. It's like riding a sofa."

A buttery three-quarter moon lit their path. When they entered the forest and its glow was extinguished, they continued in the dark. Not so long ago, the thought of entering a pitch-black wood in the small hours with her secretive grandfather would have terrified Kat. That night she felt perfectly safe. It had a lot to do with how he was around animals. She'd introduced him to Pax, who was sharing a basket with Flush in the tack room, and he and the collie had taken a shine to each other at once.

"Look at the intelligence in her eyes," he'd enthused,

wanting every detail about her background and injured paw. Kat had left out the part about how she'd plucked Pax from a dynamited cliff face. As her grandfather had talked, Flush and Faith, who'd been with him all their lives, had watched his every move with trusting brown eyes. So Kat trusted him too, though she didn't know—and he hadn't said—where they were going.

But Faith knew. The Clydesdale was alert and sure-footed on the forest path, unfazed by the snapping twigs, the whistling wind, and the owl that glided by on ghostly wings. Kat was impressed. Charming Outlaw would have bolted halfway to Scotland by now.

Twice, Kat heard hoofbeats, as if they were being shadowed by a phantom horseman, but when she looked back, there was never anyone there.

When a lake shone through the trees, her grandfather reined in Faith and helped Kat down. After tethering the horse to a tree, he guided Kat to a mound between two pines. Hidden beneath a pile of leaves was a wooden hatch, which opened to reveal concrete steps. He put a foot on the second step and held out a hand, as if nothing could be more normal than inviting his granddaughter to descend into a coffin-shaped hole in a midnight forest.

Kat hesitated on the brink, wishing that Harper, who could always be trusted to yell, "*Kat Wolfe, what the heck are you thinking?*" wasn't asleep in a far-off tower.

The Clydesdale's head shot up. She whinnied at the black trees.

"Is something out there?" Kat was thoroughly spooked.

"Come on, Katarina," her grandfather said impatiently. "It's only a squirrel."

Kat ducked down into a snug space containing a bench, cushions, and rugs, and a heap of faded, dog-eared books. It was a wildlife hide. Her grandfather set his torch on a shelf, and Kat flicked through the mini library as he arranged blankets and poured her almond-milk hot chocolate from the flask he'd made before leaving the house. Picturing her own father, Rufus, at her age, watching birds and reading *Swallows and Amazons*, *David Copperfield*, and *The Call of the Wild* made her feel closer to him than she ever had. And watching her grandfather dunk a piece of shortbread into his hot chocolate made him seem more human too.

He switched off the torch. A slim panel whirred up, exposing the lakeshore. Perched on the bench, Kat found herself with an ant's-eye view. Her grandfather tucked a blanket around her shoulders and handed her the night-vision glasses.

"Now we wait."

Kat had only ever seen one hide, which she'd visited with her class on a rainy day in East London. She'd shivered and been munched on by midges while waiting forever to see depressed ducks and a few brown birds.

Here, she was toasty in her new fleece and, thanks to the Pi-Craft binoculars, she'd be superpowered. Before she'd managed two sips of hot chocolate, a majestic stag ambled to the water's edge and drank deeply. When he raised his head and shook his antlers, sparkling droplets sent ripples rolling outward like mercury.

Kat was entranced. Fish jumped. Otters rustled in the reeds. A nightingale sang. More deer stepped daintily from the oaks.

She tried the binoculars and spotted a badger's striped snout. "Grandfather, look!" she cried. But she'd spoken too loudly. The badger retreated. Crestfallen, she watched as the deer drifted away, and the nightingale fell silent.

After that, nothing happened for an age. Kat's eyelids were drooping when her grandfather roused her.

A hare had materialized in front of the hide. It was more spirit than animal, its silhouette edged with gold moonlight, its whiskers silver. It was so near that Kat could have touched it without stretching. Confident it was safe, it began grooming itself. Nose, paws, and fluffy tail were all washed to perfection. Then, something startled it, and it was gone as if it had never been there. Kat knew she'd remember that moment all her life.

"Happy?" asked her grandfather.

Not wanting to break the spell, she could only smile and nod. For her, the best part was that the animals hadn't known she was there. It was as if she'd been given a free pass into their private world. Into her grandfather's world too.

"Your being here has given me hope, Kat," he told her. "Reminded me that there's light beyond the darkness. Oceans of it. Your being here makes the fight worth it."

A red light blinked on his watch. He cursed. In one swift motion, he pressed the button that brought down the shutter and tugged her to her feet. "Kat, the perimeter fence has been breached. Not a sound now. You must get back to the house. You'll be safe with my bodyguard."

The dark bay she'd seen racing across the field earlier was waiting beside the Clydesdale. Its boyish rider was clad in black, masked by the shifting shadows. The chauffeur had assumed its rider was probably a guest. Now it turned out that this was her grandfather's bodyguard, so clearly older than he had at first appeared. As Kat tried to grasp what was happening, her grandfather's watch flashed green. A message scrolled across the screen.

He let go of her hand. "False alarm. A bunny burrowing under a fence, apparently. Apologies for scaring you, Kat. It was always going to be a risk bringing you here. I shouldn't have done it."

"Yes, you should have," Kat declared fiercely. "I've loved every second."

The bay and the bodyguard melted away into the

forest like phantoms. It chilled her to think that they'd rehearsed the possibility of an assassin striking in this peaceful place. Or perhaps the bodyguard was always nearby. She had, after all, heard the faintest echo of hoofbeats as the Clydesdale made her way through the forest.

"Grandfather, does this happen often?" she asked. "Are you always in danger?"

"Only from rabbits! Now, Kat, shall we ask Faith if she'll carry us home? I'm not sure about you, but I could use some sleep."

HIDDEN DRAGONS

HARPER ADJUSTED HER CHAISE LOUNGE, tilted the umbrella so it shaded her laptop screen, and took a sip of fresh pineapple juice. "Okay, Kat, I'm diving in."

Kat smothered a yawn. "I thought you said the pool was too cold."

"Not *that* kind of diving," said Harper. "I'm going for a paddle in the murky currents of Johnny Roswell's life. If there are any sharks in cyberspace, they'd better watch out."

Kat lay down and covered her eyes with a baseball cap. She'd had three hours' sleep, followed by an archery lesson in the woods, a horseback tour of the estate, and a picnic hamper by a pond starred with pink water lilies. Both girls had loved the target practice and picnic, but Harper had politely declined the horse riding. Even watching Kat set out on a cheeky Welsh mountain pony gave her heart palpitations.

The Dark Lord (as Harper couldn't help thinking of him) had shown up as Kat cantered over the horizon, asking if he could interest Harper in a game of chess. She suspected he already knew that she'd been a junior chess champion in the States.

They were hunched over a board, locked in battle, when he was summoned to the north wing to see a visitor. When Harper heard Freya tell him the name of the person insisting on seeing him, he'd gripped his knight as if he might crush it.

"Forgive me, Harper," he'd said. "We must have a rematch another time." With a stiff bow, he'd stalked away, broad shoulders rigid with anger.

Freya watched him go. "I don't blame him for getting into a mood. "Sir Haslemere is being a prima donna again. Money to burn, but I've met frogs with better manners. Unfortunately, he's the prime minister's best friend and biggest donor, so His Lordship and the rest of us have no choice but to put up with him. The staff dreads his coming to stay because he always has a list of bizarre demands as long as your arm."

Harper's interest was piqued. "Such as?"

"Let me see. Once, it was a first edition of *The Hobbit*. That took some finding and cost a king's ransom. Oh, and he has an obsession with clocks. Has to have a digital one *and* an old-fashioned one for every time zone in the world, in case the power goes off. Heaven knows how he sleeps with all that ticking and blinking. Last time he came, he was thin and weak after some ghastly operation, yet he came down to breakfast the next morning looking as if he'd spent a month at a health spa."

Freya looked worried. "Forgive me, Harper—I'm not usually so indiscreet. You won't mention anything on social media, will you?"

"Never use it," Harper had assured her. "Too insecure. Scout's honor."

Now, as she sat beside the pool with Kat, who was back from her ride, Harper wondered whether there was more to the Dark Lord's dark mood than the demands of a spoiled rich man. During their game, he'd received a message that seemed to unsettle him. She'd glimpsed three words of it: *Threat Level 6.*

That told her nothing. Six could be medium or severe. And the threat could refer to almost anything. Travel in a war-torn country, or his own security. She could hardly ask him.

She was reluctant to mention it to Kat. Her best friend had been fizzing with happiness since her moonlit flit to the hide. Harper didn't want to bring her down by suggesting that there might be more to the "rabbit under the fence" incident than her grandfather had let on.

Putting it out of her mind, Harper picked up the rose-gold laptop. She was determined to make progress on their Bluebell Bay investigation.

"Do you have any questions about our latest case, Detective Wolfe? Detective Lamb will try to find the answers for you."

Kat pushed back her baseball cap. "Questions about Johnny's nonaccidental death? Yes, I do, Detective Lamb. Hundreds."

Harper's hands were poised over her keyboard. "Ready when you are, Detective Wolfe."

"What time of day was the cliff fall two years ago when Johnny was supposedly crushed by rocks?"

Harper did a search. "Easy. Around one in the morning."

Kat sat up. "When it was dark, then?"

"Uh-huh."

"Who in their right mind goes fossil hunting on cliffs in the middle of the night? Surely that proves that Johnny was murdered."

"Not necessarily," said Harper. "He might have discovered some priceless fossil and wanted to dig it up under cover of darkness."

"It would have to have been a fossil worth dying for. Or worth killing for."

"Agreed. Next question."

"Sergeant Singh said he'd found evidence that

explosives caused the cliff collapse, and I saw a flare of light over the sea when I was rescuing Pax. At the same time, you noticed the shadow of a giant shark. What if the shadow was really a gray or navy-blue boat that blended in with the sea? Or . . . is there any such thing as a glass canoe?"

Harper's fingers flew. "No glass canoes, but there's this . . ." She spun the laptop.

"A camouflage kayak! Of course. Hunters use them. So does the navy."

As she spoke, Kat was struck by a disturbing thought. On his coffee table, Mario Rossi had a photo of himself smiling atop an upturned camouflage kayak. Could he have blown up the cliff?

Sergeant Singh had told them that a possible motive for causing a landslide might be to help a local business get rich quick when the tourists came flooding in to see the exposed dinosaur or other fossils. Could Mario be in league with the owner of Taste of Tuscany, whose restaurant had been struggling due to a mouse-in-the-Parmesan incident but, thanks to the Jurassic Dragon, was now packed to the rafters every night?

Kat decided not to say anything to Harper until she was sure. She liked Mr. B and was reluctant to think that his owner might be a criminal. Innocent until proven guilty and all that.

But then a new, disquieting thought came to her.

"What if the person in the camouflage kayak first tried to dynamite the cliff two years ago, killing Johnny by accident?"

"A serial cliff-blower-upper? Seems unlikely." Harper brought up a newspaper story from the time. "Says here that that landslide was caused by days of heavy rain. The reporter describes the cliffs as being about as solid as a cookie dunked in tea. If Johnny risked his neck on them, he was either desperate to find something or he trusted the wrong person."

"Someone like his friend Harry Holt?" said Kat.

"Let's find out." Harper began typing in code. "Look away now if this makes you nervous."

"Is it legal?" fretted Kat.

"Legal schmegal," teased Harper. "I'm what's known as a white-hat hacker—always on the side of the angels."

"Who's the lucky angel today?" Kat teased back.

"Johnny's sister, JoJo. She says her brother's computer disappeared when he did. I'm going to attempt to find if there's any trace of the story he was investigating in a cloud account or file-hosting service like Dropbox."

Kat didn't look away. She couldn't. Watching Harper "walk" through walls on the internet was riveting.

The results arrived in seconds. Three links to stories about bluefin tuna located in a popular and, it turned out, not very secure, file-sharing archive.

"Tuna fish?" Kat wrinkled her nose. "I can't see Johnny being murdered over a tuna-fish sandwich."

"Or a California roll," added Harper. "Bluefin is highly prized for sushi."

She skimmed an article. "Wait, this is interesting. Ten years ago *The Independent* newspaper did a report on how a Japanese conglomerate was stockpiling hundreds of tons of bluefin in giant freezers. Yet every year, they kept buying more from across the world to sell in Tokyo fish markets."

"Bluefin tuna is one of the planet's rarest species of fish!" exclaimed Kat. "Why did the company keep fishing for more when they had tons in the freezer? Didn't they care that they were driving the bluefin out of existence?"

"Sounds as if they did care," said Harper. "But only about the money. There's another article here saying that as bluefin plunge toward extinction, their price has skyrocketed. Apparently, in January 2019, a single bluefin tuna—*one fish*—was sold for three point three million dollars in Tokyo. Some bluefin are farmed, but everyone wants to eat wild ones. I guess that means that if wild bluefin do vanish from the oceans, those in the freezers will be worth tens of millions."

Bluefin stored like gold bullion. It was a horrible thought.

Kat broke the silence. "That's sick, but I can't believe

Johnny was murdered on the Jurassic Coast because he was angry about tuna piling up in a freezer in Japan. See if you can find anything else about him."

Every search came up blank. "That doesn't make sense," said Harper, trying again. "Almost everyone leaves traces of themselves in cloud accounts. If Johnny's only footprint is three tuna stories, that's pretty fishy. Makes me wonder if his personal online history was professionally wiped."

Kat stared at her. "Could Harry have done that?"

"Nope. It would have to be someone with serious hacking skills. Someone from the intelligence services or maybe a black-hat hacker. They're criminals, by the way."

An email alert flashed across her screen. "Message from Edith. She's remembered that, as a boy, Harry hero-worshipped Mary Anning."

Kat was horizontal again. "Who?"

Harper's mouth dropped open. "You've never heard of Mary Anning, legendary nineteenth-century fossil collector? She's my hero too. She and her brother, Joseph, grew up in Lyme Regis, not far from Bluebell Bay. She was only eleven when she found her first sea dragon. That's what they called ichthyosaurs in those days.

"Back then, women were shut out of science. The best male paleontologists and museum buyers on earth made pilgrimages to Lyme Regis to buy Mary's fossils or ask for her advice. She was supposed to have been able to identify a dinosaur's exact species just from one glance at a single bone. But men took all the credit for her discoveries, and she died poor and unrecognized."

"Do you think Harry felt he was unrecognized somehow too?" asked Kat. "Edith said he taught Johnny everything he knew about fossils. If Johnny became a better collector than he was or made more money from his finds, maybe he got jealous."

Harper was reading Wikipedia. "Spooky coincidence. Harry's idol, Mary Anning, also nearly died in an 1833 landslide while out fossil hunting. It killed her dog, Tray, who went everywhere with her."

"Oh no!" cried Kat, thinking again of Pax on the cliff. "Is that why Edith emailed—to say that Mary Anning was in a landslide too?"

"No, she wanted to tell us about an article Harry wrote for a science magazine a few years ago on Mary Anning. He was devastated when it was rejected and showed Edith the letter from the editor. He didn't want it back. She's attached it here in case it's significant."

Dear Mr. Holt,

Thank you for submitting your article "Mary Anning's Lost Letters" to *Fossils*

Forever. If we specialized in pulp
fiction, it would make for fun reading,
but we are a serious scientific journal.

It is preposterous to suggest, without
evidence, that the great Mary Anning
hinted at "dragons" concealed beneath
the cliffs at Bluebell Bay, or that the
letters that might prove your claim
were stolen over a century ago by the
fantastically named Order of Dragons.

If I published your conspiracy
theories, I'd be laughed out of town. I
wish you the best in your future career
as a novelist.

Regretfully,
Walter Block
Editor in Chief

Kat said tiredly, "Everywhere we turn, there are
dragons. What's the Order of Dragons, Detective
Lamb?"

But as Harper hit ENTER on the search, a flashing
scarlet banner filled her screen.

ACCESS TO THIS SITE IS RESTRICTED.
PROCEEDING MAY RESULT IN CRIMINAL

PROSECUTION AND THE CONFISCATION OF ANY
AND ALL COMPUTER DEVICES.

Hastily, she shut the page. "Whoa, that was unexpected. Guess we won't be finding out about the Order of Dragons anytime soon."

Kat shut her eyes. "Can't say I'm sorry. I've had all the dragons I can take for one day." She was asleep in seconds.

It was hot enough to bake a cake on the pool deck. Without a device to divert her, Harper was bored and restless. She picked up Kat's mystery novel but was too agitated to focus. The minister of defense had entrusted her with his spare laptop. What if she'd brought trouble to his door by accessing an illegal site? Kat would never forgive her.

She was about to wake Kat when a disembodied voice thundered, "Don't you just *loathe* children? So sticky, smelly, and unruly."

It took Harper a moment to work out where it was coming from. There was an air vent in the tiles beneath her chaise lounge. Below it was the basement gym in the north wing. A conversation rose up clearly through an iron grille. As far as she could tell, the men were by the indoor pool.

A second speaker said, "I have three children of my own. I must say, I'm rather fond of them."

"*Three!* However do you cope? I suppose you have nannies. Apologies for any offense. It's just that apart from their hygiene, or lack of it, kids have this disturbing way about them. It's as if they *see* things."

There was a throaty chuckle. "See into your soul, you mean? Have you dusted the cobwebs off yours recently?"

"Very funny. There's this boy—the son of a . . . business acquaintance. He's up to something, I just know it. He has this watchful quality about him, like he's scheming. No matter. When the boy and his dad have outlived their usefulness, they'll be eliminated."

Goose bumps rose on Harper's arms. It sounded like a Level 10 threat, not a joke.

The man continued: "As I was saying, Hamilton Park is the last place one would expect to see kids, but there are two here. Who do they belong to? Any chance we can evict them?"

"Good luck with that. His Lordship's granddaughter and her friend are staying. From what I've heard, he dotes on Katarina."

"Ah, yes, I forgot he has a tiresome weakness for children and animals. Do you recall the time he banned us from using that terrace for three months because the swifts were nesting? But I digress. I'm putting in a new order tomorrow. Want anything?"

"Certainly do. My arthritis has been playing up. Two black T-shirts for me, and a striped one for my wife.

She's redecorating. If there's any white plastic available, I'd like to order a fancy carving for her birthday."

"Consider it done."

Harper's curiosity got the better of her. She slid the chaise lounge aside and put an eye to the grille. All she could see was the shoes of one of the men. Black brogues with sky-blue laces.

"Who are you spying on?" inquired Kat.

Harper jerked up guiltily, bumping the table. A full pitcher of pineapple juice tipped over and poured through the grille.

"What the . . . ?" spluttered one man. "Is someone up there?"

"Kat, code red! Code red!" whispered Harper, which was their agreed way of communicating an emergency requiring action first, questions later.

Snatching up the book, laptop, and towels, they sprinted past the tennis courts and through an archway that led to the south wing. Only when they were safely in the tower room did Harper realize she'd left her sunglasses beside the pool.

KILLER MOVES

THAT NIGHT, KAT DREAMED SHE WAS LOST in the Hamilton Park maze. Tiny was there as well. Yet no matter how swiftly she ran or how loudly she called, he was always just out of reach, his stripy tail slipping around the next bend in the yew hedge. Then his tail morphed into a scaly red dragon. When it turned on Kat, blasting flames in her direction, it wore a mask.

"Coward!" she screamed silently. "Show yourself! Who are you?"

"You're burning up," said Harper, shaking her out of the nightmare. "It might be sunstroke or flu. I'm calling Freya or your granddad."

"No, don't!" Kat didn't want a fuss. She wanted to be back in her own bed in her own home, ideally with her cat cuddled up beside her. If she could have fled the creaking manor, with its unsmiling portraits and shifty guests, now, in the middle of the night, she would have packed her bags without hesitation.

It didn't take a psychologist to spell out why she was having bad dreams. She was anxious about Tiny. On the face of it, she had nothing to be concerned about. If Dr. Wolfe's texts were to be believed, Tiny was fine, Xena was fine, Janey's cat was fine, Charming Outlaw was fine, and so was Orkaan. That was the problem. There were too many fines. It made Kat suspicious.

How is everything at Hamilton Park? her mum had texted.

Fine! wrote Kat.

And how are you getting on with your grandfather?
Fine!

Two could play at that game.

Nurse Tina had been more forthcoming:

Xena is quite the diva. Insists on sharing my pillow. As for my sneakers, the left is no more. Luckily, I was planning to replace them anyway. P.S. Come home soon. Tiny misses you.

In the tower room, Kat gave Harper a hug. "Thanks for saving me from the dragon. If you hadn't woken me, it would have swallowed me whole."

Harper grinned. "You're welcome. What are best friends for if not to save each other from dragons?"

Kat's heart rate returned to normal. First thing in the morning, the chauffeur was due to return them to Bluebell Bay. She'd be reunited with Tiny by midday at the latest. Everything really would be fine. All she had to do was survive till then.

She pushed back the duvet. "Freya told me we could help ourselves to hot chocolate from the kitchen any time. Fancy some?"

Harper climbed out of bed. "Sure! I'll come with you."

Kat had hoped that her grandfather would be in his study when they passed on their way to the kitchen. She really wanted to talk to him. Tiny wasn't the only thing weighing on her mind. The missing dragon card was also bothering her . . .

Earlier that evening, before dinner, Kat had been saying good night to the horses when she'd heard a cat meowing in the stable hayloft. Checking on it had been her first mistake. Her second had been not leaving once she'd spotted the hammock strung up between the beams. There was also a camping stove, tinned food, a stuffed rucksack, and a pile of books on a hay bale. It was the books that were Kat's undoing. The moment she'd spotted *The Way of the Mongoose: Twenty-Five Killer Moves*, she'd pounced on it.

The Way of the Mongoose was an obscure martial art originating in Shanghai, China. Kat had spent months trying to teach herself a few of its 113 throws and blocks. All the experts were agreed that reading *Killer Moves* was a fast track to becoming a Mongoose master. Unfortunately, it was out of print. Instinctively, Kat knew that this copy belonged to the rider of the bay horse. The mere idea that her grandfather's protector might be a Mongoose master was thrilling beyond measure.

But the bodyguard's living quarters raised uncomfortable questions. Why was he banished to the stables rather than enjoying the spacious staff quarters? Did her grandfather treat his workers cruelly?

There'd been no one else around. The head groom, James, was out feeding the sheep and had taken the dogs with him. After flipping through the book, Kat had decided to try out Move 18: the Butterfly Sweep.

As she'd fought off an imaginary assailant—taking him down by shoving his right knee with one foot while sweeping away his left ankle—the black-and-gold dragon card had flown out of her polo-shirt pocket and fallen through a gap in the hayloft floorboards. Kat had watched it land beside a water trough below. She'd replaced the book and shinnied down the ladder to retrieve it.

But the card was gone.

Kat had stared at the concrete in disbelief. There were no similar water troughs or drains into which it could have fallen. After checking the tack room and stalls for signs of life, she'd run to the stable block entrance. The only person in sight had been a gardener pruning a wisteria near the north wing. But unless he'd mastered time travel, he couldn't have run across the lawn and found the card in the minute it had taken Kat to descend the ladder.

"Lost something?" James had asked, coming in with the border collies at his heels to find Kat crawling around on the stable floor.

"Only Pax. I was missing her." Kat was unwilling to admit to losing an unidentified and possibly valuable card that didn't belong to her. "Here, Pax girl. Give me a cuddle. Did you have fun with the sheep? Uh, James, were you just in here?"

"Think I could have snuck in here with this lively pair without you noticing? Not likely. By the way, I'll be away for the night staying with my mum. One of our gardeners will be taking care of Pax and Flush."

Kat had nodded vaguely, still thinking about the card. The most obvious thief was the bodyguard, who was adept at coming and going like a ghost. But if he'd seen the card fall, why hadn't he called out to her? Why snatch it unless he knew something about the dragon card that Kat didn't? Was it a special credit card from one of those banks that only accepted money from billionaires and famous people such as the Swanns? If it *did* belong to the actors or another wealthy hotel guest, would they soon find their accounts emptied out?

"James, who lives in the hayloft?" Kat had asked.

James turned on a tap and noisily filled two buckets. "His Lordship invited a horse trainer he knows to come and work with our yearlings for a couple of weeks."

Kat found it curious that the groom was unaware that the mystery man was actually His Lordship's bodyguard. "Why isn't the trainer staying in the manor?" she'd pressed. "It's not like there's a shortage of bedrooms."

"V doesn't do walls," James said matter-of-factly.

"V as in Vee? Or is V short for Vincent or Vaughan or something?" Kat had wanted to know.

But James, clanking away with the buckets, hadn't answered.

CROUCHING TIGERS

AT DINNER, KAT HAD BEEN IN A DILEMMA. Her grandfather had gone to great lengths to ensure that she and Harper had the best time possible at Hamilton Park. She didn't want to ruin their last supper together by making accusations of theft against V, who'd been ready to whisk her to safety if the rabbit under the fence had in fact been an assassin.

"Why don't you simply describe the dragon card to your granddad and ask if he's ever seen one like it?" Harper had suggested. "That way, you're not accusing anyone of taking it. He might say, 'Oh, an estate worker handed it in,' or even recognize it as a squillionaire's bank card, or a membership pass to a posh London club. My guess is that it's a gift card for a shop that sells dragon toys and books. The thief will be lucky if it has five pounds on it."

In any event, Kat never had the chance to raise the subject. Some crisis had erupted in the Dark Lord's world, and he'd been pulled away from the table three times before disappearing altogether.

He'd apologized and made light of it when he came to say good night later. Kat hadn't believed a word of it. If everything was so hunky-dory, why were two armed guards with bulging muscles suddenly patrolling the grounds?

Perhaps sensing her anxiety, he'd said unexpectedly, "You mustn't be afraid, Kat Wolfe. Even dragons have their ending."

Even dragons have their ending.

His words came back to Kat now as she and Harper stood at his study door shortly after 1 A.M. Moonlight fell on the Persian carpet, which had been moved aside. Did her grandfather have insomnia again? Had he gone to visit his Clydesdale?

"Is that the trapdoor you were telling me about?" whispered Harper. "I've never been in a secret tunnel before. Any chance I could see it? We could go to the stable and have another hunt for the dragon card."

Kat thought that was an excellent plan. If her grandfather was there, he might take Harper to see the deer and hare too. She brought along the night-vision glasses just in case.

But when they pushed up through the straw into

Faith's stall, the stable block was in darkness. Kat let down the trapdoor behind them and listened. The horses were pacing and snorting uneasily, their ears flickering like radar detectors.

If something was wrong, why weren't the dogs barking? Then she remembered that Pax and Flush were spending the night with one of the gardeners. "Harper, I have a bad feeling. We should get back."

Harper squeezed her arm. A dark figure was passing the dusty stable window.

They ducked down and heard nothing further. Harper gestured at the trapdoor, but Kat whispered, "Too risky. It squeaks. Stay here with Faith. I'll wake the bodyguard."

Soundlessly she unbolted the stall door and scaled the hayloft ladder. At the top, she blinked in shock. Every trace of the bodyguard and his hammock, books, and camping stove had gone. Were it not for a stray striped sock, he might have been a figment of Kat's imagination. She tucked the sock into her pocket as proof that she hadn't made it all up.

Harper was waiting at the bottom of the ladder. She steered Kat to the window. "Look."

An intruder was on the roof of the manor house, moving audaciously toward the south wing. Three stories below, an armed guard rounded the front of the house and strolled along the gravel path, yawning and stretching. Kat lifted the night-vision glasses. Another figure was on the roof, stalking the first. It was V, the bodyguard. She was sure of it.

Sensing someone behind him, the intruder let fly with a roundhouse karate kick. The bodyguard countered with what Kat identified as Move 10: the Leaping Tiger. The guard crossed the driveway below. He bent to smell a rose, oblivious to the drama unfolding on the rooftop. The fighters were so graceful, it was hard to believe they were fighting. It was more ballet than brawl. Their silhouettes were outlined against the stars, soaring, spinning, and blocking.

"Should we try to get the guard's attention?" Harper whispered.

But he was too far away to hear them shout, and Kat was nervous that he might shoot them if they startled him. And she didn't want to endanger V, battling on the roof.

As the guard passed the maze and was lost to view, the intruder performed a dizzying leap off the roof and rappelled down the side of the south wing. V, up there with no rope, watched him bolt away into the darkness.

"Let's get out of here," said Kat.

Harper didn't argue. They shot back along the secret passage and up to the tower room. Harper dived gratefully into her safe, warm bed. "Should we wake anyone?"

Downstairs, a phone trilled, a door opened, and hushed, urgent voices echoed up the stairwell.

"I think we'd only be in the way," said Kat, wishing again that she was at home with Tiny, who protected her the way V protected her grandfather.

Adrenaline was charging through her veins, and she was sure that she'd lie awake till morning, but she was asleep in seconds, with the Dark Lord's words running through her head: *You mustn't be afraid, Kat Wolfe. Even dragons have their ending.*

ANIMAL CONTROL

AT NINE ON THE DOT, THEY LEFT HAMILTON Park in a limousine driven by a different chauffeur, this one courteous but tight-lipped. There was no ginger beer. The bulletproof screen that separated him from his passengers also ensured there'd be no laughs.

As the iron gates and snarling lions faded into the distance behind them, Kat exhaled.

"Sorry, Harper—it wasn't quite the relaxing *Downton Abbey* weekend I promised."

"Are you kidding? It's the most fun I've had in ages! I can't wait to visit again . . . But what did you make of what Freya said at breakfast?"

They'd come down to find Freya humming cheerfully over pancakes in the kitchen, Kat's grandfather long gone.

"His Lordship said to wish you both a safe trip back to Bluebell Bay. Duty called, I'm afraid."

Kat hadn't been surprised. "A situation?"

Freya laughed. "How did you guess? Sleep well?"

Harper poured herself some orange juice. "Yes, thanks—although we heard some strange noises. We were scared it might be a burglar."

"No such luck," said Freya, putting maple syrup on the table. "His Lordship and I keep hoping that someone will break in and steal that dreadful painting of his grouse-shooting Great-Uncle Horace, but it hasn't happened yet. Kat, there's coconut yogurt if you'd like some. No, the guards reported a peaceful night."

"Do you think Freya was lying or genuinely didn't have the faintest idea that there'd been an intruder on the roof?" asked Harper now as the limo picked up speed.

"She doesn't seem like the lying kind," said Kat, lowering the window so that Pax could watch the country lanes whip by. "Not unless it's a matter of national security, which it might be. After all, someone—presumably his bodyguard—woke my grandfather and told him about it. What I'm curious about is why no alarms sounded. It would have been nice if my grandfather had come to check on us, but maybe he assumed we were okay in the tower room and didn't want to worry us."

"Maybe," Harper said doubtfully. "I did enjoy it, but

I'm sort of relieved to be heading home. Life seems a lot simpler in Bluebell Bay. Or it did before the dinosaur discovery, anyway. Which reminds me, Detective Wolfe, we need to get on with our case."

Kat took out her notebook. "Why don't we start now?"

She wrote *WHO KILLED JOHNNY?* on a page and drew two columns.

SUSPECT	MOTIVE
Harry Holt	Jealousy or greed over Johnny discovering a priceless fossil
Rival fossil hunter	Ditto
Environment-destroying company (e.g., weed-killer maker, foxhunters, badger murderers, tree choppers)	Fear of evil deeds being exposed
The "monsters" Johnny was investigating	Ditto

"All we ever get is more questions" was Kat's glum verdict.

"We do know one thing," said Harper. "Johnny told his sister that he was investigating monsters. Not *a* monster. Monsters *plural*. Two or more. I vote that we cross Harry off our suspect list altogether. He wouldn't have told Edith that they didn't like what Johnny was doing, so they 'put a stop to it' if he was talking about himself, would he? Anyway, I think we're fairly certain that the tree choppers, foxhunters, and badger murderers didn't kill him. That shortens our suspect list."

Kat nodded. "I agree about the tree choppers, foxhunters, and badger murderers, but Harry is still an unknown quantity. He could have been working with someone else—a fellow collector. The *Fossils Forever* editor made fun of Harry's claims that Mary Anning wrote about 'dragons' hidden under the cliffs at Bluebell Bay. What if two years ago, Harry and Johnny were competing to be the first to find the Jurassic Dragon?"

Harper said excitedly, "What if someone else beat them to it?" Then, less excitedly, "I guess they couldn't have, though, because the dracoraptor was found only a week ago. But that doesn't mean that a rival collector didn't keep hunting for it. We need to find out if the Order of Dragons still exists. It could be a secret society like the Masons that's gone on and on through the centuries."

As the limousine crossed into Dorset, Kat said, "Maybe we should start looking into some of the mini mysteries we keep stumbling across. One or two of them might be connected."

"Mini mysteries?"

"The ones that sound like Enid Blyton novels. We have *The Order of Dragons Mystery* and *The Disappearing*

Dragon Card Mystery and *The Mystery of the Intruder on the Roof.* Oh, and *The Mystery of the Phantom Bodyguard.*"

Harper giggled. "Then there's *The Coded Conversation Mystery.* I'm sure that's what I overheard at Hamilton Park—government officials or possibly visitors talking in code. Otherwise, the stuff about striped T-shirts and white plastic carvings doesn't make an ounce of sense. And I wish I knew more about *The Father and Son Mystery.* The ones who were going to be eliminated when they'd outlived their usefulness."

Kat chewed the top of her pen. "Do you think that was code for something too?"

"Hope so—but what if it wasn't? The man sounded deadly serious. Do you think it's worth reporting it to your granddad?"

"Let's see if we can find out more on our own first. You said one of the men wore blue shoelaces. We could try looking up companies that sell blue laces. Maybe they're made by an exclusive designer shoe shop with only a few customers."

"I wish," Harper said wryly. "I did a search and got five-hundred-thousand results."

Kat closed the limousine window. Using Pax's back as a desk, she made a circle of balloons around the edge of a page. "If we put names, places, and clues in each of these and draw strings between the ones that have something in common, we might see an unexpected connection."

"Smart thinking. Can you add *The Mystery of Why the Swanns Are in Bluebell Bay* and *The Mystery of Who Bought Ollie Merriweather Lobster and Champagne?*"

"If we also include *The Mystery of Who Blew Up the Cliff* and *The Mystery of Who Killed Johnny Roswell*, we have ten mini mysteries," said Kat. *"Ten."*

"Then we'd better get to work," Harper responded happily. "Mysteries don't solve themselves!"

By the time the limousine crested the hill above Bluebell Bay, they'd found a few connections—mostly to do with the Grand Hotel Majestic, dragons, and the dinosaur. Nothing sinister leaped out at them. Kat tucked her notebook away. When she saw the sparkling cove, the clouds that had swirled around her since she'd dropped the dragon card lifted.

Paradise House was on the outskirts of the town, so they stopped there first.

"Hello, Trouble . . . and Kat!" cried Nettie as she opened the door. "We've missed you both so much—haven't we, Bailey?"

The parrot flew to Harper's shoulder and rubbed his cheek against hers, crooning, "'Here's looking at you, kid.'"

While Nettie made the chauffeur a coffee to go, Kat ran to the stable yard to see Charming Outlaw and

Orkaan. She was taken aback when she noticed Outlaw's bridle slung carelessly over a hook, salty with sweat and broken.

After giving the horses treats and pats, she ran to ask the housekeeper what had happened.

"Oh, about that. Ethan Swann turned up to ride on Saturday morning, not long after you and Harper left for Hamilton Park. He asked if we'd mind if he rode Charming Outlaw rather than his own black mare. Said you'd been keen to persuade him that our chestnut race-horse was even faster than the horse in his last film. I didn't think Harper would mind him riding her horse, so of course I said yes. Doesn't he have the dreamiest blue eyes? Ethan, that is, not the racehorse."

Kat was furious but couldn't decide who was at fault—the actor for twisting her words, or herself for boasting about Charming Outlaw in a way that made Ethan covet Harper's horse. "How did the reins get broken?"

"The horse took fright at a rabbit. Ethan was very sorry and sweetly said we must add a brand-new bridle to the final tab."

After Kat said goodbye to Harper, the limo driver took Kat home. She was still thinking dark thoughts about the Swanns' ever-growing bill and how rabbits seemed to be a convenient excuse for everything from intruders to poor horsemanship when they turned onto Summer Street. A white van with ANIMAL CONTROL on the side was parked next to number 5. Her mum was arguing with someone on the lawn.

Kat had the door open before the car had come to a halt. "Mum, what's happening? Where's Tiny?"

Her mum gave an imperceptible shake of her head. Over the stranger's shoulder, Kat saw Tiny jump over the neighbor's fence. She had to restrain herself from rushing to him.

Dr. Wolfe said, "Darling, this is Mr. Bludger, an animal control officer from the council. I'm sorry to greet you with bad news. Unfortunately, there's been another case of sheep worrying. We've had a call from Wiley Evans, who has the farm on the hill. His wife saw a cat matching Tiny's description shortly before the sheep was attacked last night."

Mr. Bludger said, "Two farmers have ID'd your Savannah as the culprit."

"But that's impossible, Mum," cried Kat. "Tiny was here with you and Tina, wasn't he?"

Her mum didn't reply. She said, "I've already told Mr. Bludger that no domestic cat—even a half-wild one as big as Tiny—could have inflicted those injuries on a sheep. Mr. Bludger, I must ask you to—"

"There's the beast!" The animal control officer pointed a pudgy finger in triumph. Tiny was striding across the lawn, green eyes fixed on Kat. "If you grab it, I'll get the trap out of the van. You'll have the right to appeal, Dr. Wolfe, but I wouldn't waste your time or money. Far as I'm concerned, it's a cut-and-dried case. Get a Burmese next. They're easier to manage."

It was like being caught in the maze nightmare again. Kat wanted to scream, but no sound came out.

Before anyone could move, there was a joyful yelp. Spotting Tiny, Pax bounded out of the chauffeur's grasp and raced to greet her feline friend. At the exact same moment, Xena came flying out of the house, yapping with delight at the sight of Kat. Tiny fled with a yowl. Kat wasn't sure whether to laugh or cry.

Mr. Bludger was livid. "I'll be back. Until then, I'm revoking your cat's F1 Savannah license; see if you think that's funny. As of this minute, he's a wanted cat with a bounty on his head."

Dr. Wolfe held Kat tightly as they watched the taillights of first the limousine and then the animal control van, fade away down Summer Street.

"Tiny is innocent," she said. "You know it, and I know it. I can't deny he was out wandering last night, but he didn't do what they're accusing him of. We'll order a DNA test to prove it if necessary. Trust me, Kat, we'll save Tiny. You can count on it."

OUTCASTS AND ANGELS

"I DON'T UNDERSTAND WHY SHE HAS TO sit outside *my* window," moaned Margo Truesdale, proprietor of the Jurassic Fantastic Deli, lips puckering as if she'd sucked an extra-sour sherbet lemon. "She's driving away business. There must be a hundred other places she can go. The Outer Hebrides, for example. But if she must come to Bluebell Bay, why can't she sit elsewhere? I think I'll suggest that she'll be more comfortable on the bench in front of the Sea Breeze Tea Room."

"Don't do that; they might offer her one of their scones," said a customer. "The plain ones are dry enough to choke a horse. As for their tea, I'd rather drink brine from a jar of pickled onions."

To begin with, Kat was only half listening as she

stood at the deli counter watching the oven timer tick down on the mushroom pie she was collecting for dinner.

"Mind you don't come home with a boxful of crumbs," Nurse Tina had kidded as she'd left the house. Everyone knew that Kat could not be trusted with warm bakery goods.

Kat had made no promises. She was starving, having eaten nothing since she'd gotten back from Hamilton Park that morning because she'd felt so ill about Tiny. He'd come strolling in at midday, unaware that there was a £1,000 bounty on his head. Once he was sure that Pax wasn't about to ambush him, his swagger had returned. When Kat had scooped him up, he'd purred like a panther.

"Lock him in your room till morning," her mum had instructed. "Strictly speaking, it's illegal for us to keep an unlicensed F1 Savannah, a virtual wildcat, but what choice do we have? The only way for us to clear Tiny's name is to keep him hidden until whatever creature is attacking the sheep reveals itself or strikes again. Then Mr. Bludger will have to eat his words. In the meantime, I'll keep Pax in the kennels. She won't be happy about it, but we'll give her lots of love and attention, and you can take her for short walks."

On the way to the deli, Kat had swung by the Grand

Hotel Majestic to drop off Xena. Ethan had answered the door with an ice pack pressed to one eye. He'd lifted it to show a dark bruise and swollen cheekbone.

"Great look for a movie actor, huh? People keep giving Alicia funny stares, but the truth is kinda boring. I had an argument with the corner of the wardrobe."

Kat opened her mouth to speak, but he was already shutting her out.

"My wife's not here. I'll tell her you stopped by. Adios, Kat. We'll be in touch."

Ethan's black eye and the way he'd clutched at his ribs after leaning down to pat Xena only fueled Kat's suspicions that Charming Outlaw had thrown him. No wonder he'd been in such a hurry to get rid of Kat—he didn't want any awkward questions. If she ever got up the nerve, Kat planned to ask him why he'd hired Orkaan from Pet Performers if he had no intention of riding her. Was the Friesian mare purely for show, like the Aston Martin? Was she nothing more than a living prop to put on Instagram?

Now, as Kat waited at the counter for the pie to emerge from the oven, her thoughts returned to Tiny. He hated being cooped up, and thanks to heartless Mr. Bludger, he was a refugee locked indefinitely in her bedroom.

Kat tried to decide which Mongoose Move would be most effective if the animal control officer ever tried to drag Tiny into his rusty trap. The Butterfly Sweep was not as dramatic as Move 10: the Leaping Tiger—a technique used by the bodyguard on the roof of Hamilton Park—but it was a good choice for a girl fighting off an adult two or three times her height or weight.

She was mentally rehearsing it when a snippet of conversation caught her ear.

"Doesn't Sergeant Singh care if we're all murdered in our beds?" said a woman at a nearby table.

Her friend leaned forward conspiratorially. "The way my niece tells it—she's a police photographer—he didn't feel he had a choice. Harry Holt keeps confessing to murder, but he won't say why or how he did it. And the forensics prove that Johnny died accidentally. Sergeant Singh thinks Harry is only saying he did it because he feels safer in jail than wandering around Bluebell Bay. He seems petrified of someone but won't say who. Keeps telling Singh, 'They're out there. They'll get me.'"

"*Who's* out there?"

"Aliens, most probably. Hopefully, the police psychologist will get to the bottom of it. Harry's seeing her tomorrow. If he's judged sane, he'll be released onto the streets."

The oven timer pinged, and the girl behind the counter took down a large box to put Kat's pie in. Behind her, the customer was still fuming about Harry's possible release.

"We should start a petition to keep him locked up forever. One only has to look at his hair to tell that he's as mad as a box of frogs. We don't need those sorts of people in Bluebell Bay."

"You can't lock people up for having bad hair," the woman with the police photographer niece was saying. "If that were a valid criterion, my daughter would be in solitary confinement. I confess that, before this happened, I liked Harry a lot. He was so kind and helpful. I can't think what's happened to make him so afraid."

"What's turned him into a killer, you mean," retorted the other woman. "*I'm* the one who'll be afraid if he's out on the streets again."

"Anything else?" the waitress asked Kat.

Simmering with silent anger on Harry's behalf, Kat stared at her blankly. "Excuse me?"

"Would you like anything else?"

"Sorry, no—just the pie. Thanks."

Kat fumbled for the cash her mum had given her. She tuned back in to the conversation dominating the diner while she waited for her change.

"She's putting people off their food," grumbled Margo to a tourist in a Jurassic Dragon T-shirt. "People feel guilty eating at my outdoor tables with her sitting there, judging them."

"Let's call the council. Maybe they have a space in a hostel."

The waitress was back. "Sorry for the wait, Kat— here's your change." She called to her boss. "Margo, I think I saw that *X Factor* star go by. What's he called again? The one who used to be a builder. He was going to come in, but he saw the homeless woman and veered off up the street."

Outside, the target of their displeasure was sitting in the sunshine on a grass mat. A much-mended Indian shirt and ancient ripped jeans clung to her lanky frame. Mismatched socks were bunched in boots with holes in both soles. Long wiry gray hair hung past a deeply tanned face, with eyes as watchful as a wildcat's. The woman seemed as coiled as one too. Yet when Margo advanced on her, she didn't stir.

Kat put the pie box on an empty outdoor table. She watched with growing dismay as Margo and her supporters tried to force the woman to move on. The deli owner started off syrupy sweet before moving on to bribery.

"If I give you ten pounds and a slice of chocolate cake, perhaps you could enjoy lunch in the park?" Margo was becoming increasingly annoyed by the woman's stubbornness. "If you don't leave now, I'm calling the police," she threatened. "There've been complaints about your patchouli oil. You're putting people off their food."

"This is all the fault of the stupid Jurassic Dragon," commented one bystander. "It's filled Bluebell Bay with undesirables."

"Leave her alone!" said Kat in a small voice, but a bottleneck of shoppers and eaters and rubberneckers had built up in the cobbled street. Nobody heard her above the buzz.

Something in Kat snapped. She thought of Tiny, condemned to an animal prison just because he was big and looked feral, and about the rich daughter who'd rejected Pax and possibly flung her from a car. And she thought with shame about how she herself had rushed to judge Harry as a murderer based on his unkempt curls and jam-stained shirt.

"LEAVE HER ALONE!" she shouted.

The gathered throng turned as one, astonishment on their faces.

"How would you like it if you had no home and no one cared for you and people judged you just because you couldn't get to a shower or didn't match up with what someone on social media thought was okay?" Kat could feel her cheeks burning. "How would you feel if people were cruel to you and put a bounty on your head?"

"Kat, no one's saying anything about a bounty," Margo blustered. "We're merely saying that Bluebell Bay is a nice town with nice people and has a certain reputation—"

"Yes, Bluebell Bay is the most perfect town in the whole universe, except for the people who are mean to anyone who doesn't fit their perfect picture, or who want to lock animals in cages when their only crime is looking different. Who makes the rules, anyway?"

Margo was looking uncomfortable. "I don't know what you mean. What rules?"

"Who's the judge of who's perfect and who isn't? You? Sergeant Singh? The editor of the local newspaper?"

"The girl's right," said the baker, who'd come out to see what the fuss was about. "What harm is the woman doing anyway? She's enjoying the sunshine and minding her own business."

A family of tourists agreed. They raided their wallets, and others joined them to fill the woman's hat with change.

Kat pushed her way to the front of the crowd. The homeless woman scrambled to her feet, clutching her bedroll. She had dolphin eyes, as clear as the sky.

Kat said gently, "Would you like to come home with me for dinner? It's just me—I'm Kat—and my mum and Tina. My mum's a vet, and Tina's her nurse, and they won't mind at all if you join us. We have a huge pie for our supper, and you'd be very welcome . . ."

The woman murmured, "This wasn't how it was supposed to be."

"Kat!" cried Margo. "Your pie!"

"Or if you'd prefer," Kat pressed on, "I can give you the whole pie, and you can eat it wherever you're comfortable. It's vegan, if that's okay."

The homeless woman pushed up her sleeves, revealing a tattoo of an angel on her right forearm. But it was the tattoo on the left that caused Kat to stare. It was a mongoose facing down a cobra.

"Hey, Kat," said a boy she knew from school, poking her in the ribs. "You might want to check out your pie."

Kat wrenched her gaze from the tattoo in time to see a seagull making off with a choice morsel. She dashed to the box, but there was nothing left but crumbs.

Tearfully, she turned to apologize to the woman for offering her a pie that no longer existed, but she'd already fled, leaving behind the hatful of money. Kat looked up and down the street, but there was no trace of her. And before she could think more about the woman's strange remark—*This wasn't how it was supposed to be*—she saw Ollie Merriweather, Professor Lamb's assistant, arguing on a street corner with the rude man from the hotel. The same man who'd told her he knew nothing about the gold-and-black dragon card but might actually have been the one who owned it.

"Kat Wolfe?" The mother from the caravan park, the one whose daughter had fallen in love with Xena, was smiling down at her. "I saw what you just did. I'm sorry about your pie, but if you'd allow me, I'd like to buy you and your family another. I haven't forgotten your kindness to Immie. If I can make it up to you, I'd like to."

That was the thing about humans, thought Kat. Just when you were all ready to give up on them, they turned around and surprised you.

BONE WARS

"NO PRIZES FOR GUESSING HOW THE burglar broke in," said Harper, standing on tiptoe to inspect the jagged hole in the window of the old hall. "Where was Mike when the intruder was smashing the pane with a rock? On the phone to his mother? Playing video games?"

"Mike wasn't on guard duty last night," her father said tiredly. It was seven o'clock on Tuesday morning, and he'd been up since four thirty. "We have a new man, Bash. It's not his fault. He's highly experienced and came with glowing references. Unluckily, he was answering a call of nature when the thief struck."

"Must have been a long call," quipped Levi, one of the volunteers. "The thief had to get in and out. Did Bash eat a bad prawn?"

Professor Lamb ignored him. He crunched over

broken glass to the main hall, where disheveled and yawning volunteers and students, one still in his pajamas, were gathering around the coffee urn. Eleven chairs had been put out for them.

Kat came in with the last of the volunteers, breathing hard after racing down the hill. **URGENT!** Harper had texted. **Break-in at the old hall! Need your eyes and ears. Could be connected to our case. Come—but be invisible.**

Kat slipped in almost unnoticed and took a seat on a pile of dusty cloths. She was all but hidden by a table. Harper stood with her father and Bash, the new security guard, before the semicircle of chairs.

Professor Lamb said, "Many of you will be wondering why I haven't called the police. First, Sergeant Singh is working round the clock on a murder inquiry that started in this very building with the discovery of Johnny Roswell's remains. I don't want to bother him unnecessarily."

"If parts of one of the rarest dinosaurs in Britain have been stolen, it's an emergency!" cried a concerned student. "*I'll* call the police if you won't."

Professor Lamb lifted a hand. "Thanks, Tibor, but you might want to hear me out. It's my belief that the robbery was an inside job."

Ollie leaped to his feet. "Are you saying you don't trust us—your own team?"

"Sit down, Oliver. I'm saying that I'm giving the

thief a chance to do the right thing before I involve the police. I've asked my daughter to be here because Harper's both an insider and an outsider. She's grown up around fossils and paleontologists, but she's not in the business and often sees things I miss. If whoever has stolen the Jurassic Dragon's teeth comes forward now, they have my word they'll face no consequences."

A buzz went through the room. Kat noticed that beneath his chair, Ollie's boots jiggled furiously.

"Why don't we check the CCTV?" he said. "I wager that everyone in this room will be in the clear."

"We have studied the CCTV," Professor Lamb told him. "Someone set the video to play on a loop last night. For nearly twelve hours, Bash here was watching what appeared to be an empty hall."

"Why would any of us risk ruining our reputation to steal a few teeth?" asked Samira, a fresh-faced geology student.

Professor Lamb shrugged. "Why does anyone steal anything? Greed? Desperation?"

"I can't believe you're accusing us after all we've done for you," Ollie said angrily. "This is an outrage."

Theo Lamb looked sad. "Is it, Ollie? Well, it's easy enough to prove. As you know, I'm a technical dunce, but my daughter takes after her mom. Harper could code by the time she could walk. Over the past week,

I've been besieged with calls offering me a fortune to sell off bits of the Jurassic Dragon. I'm aware that many of you have too. To be on the safe side, I asked Harper to help me set up extra security cameras. Let's take a look at them now."

Harper started to project a video onto the wall of the hall. As the crew watched, a figure in a black hoody was seen slipping through the unguarded gate seconds after Bash had scuttled to the bathroom. Kat studied the crew as they viewed the footage. On the film, the grainy burglar broke the window with a gloved hand and went directly to the drawer where the smaller fossils were kept. Using a penknife to pry the drawer open, he pocketed a pouch. As he spun to leave, a streetlight revealed his face.

There was no mistaking Oliver Merriweather.

A fight broke out as the crew turned on Professor Lamb's assistant.

"How could you betray us like that, Ollie?"

"What sort of person lies about being innocent while his friends and colleagues are accused of stealing?"

"How could you sell off something so priceless for profit?"

Ollie sagged in his chair as if he wished a sinkhole would swallow him, all his bravado gone. With his hair flopping over his pale face, he was like a toddler caught red-handed with a pocketful of sweets. "I didn't do it," he half sobbed. "I didn't steal the dinosaur's teeth."

"Stop lying! It's there in black and white."

"Harper," he begged, "fast-forward the video to around two A.M."

The crew watched as Ollie broke back into the hall about forty minutes after snatching the dragon's teeth and replaced the pouch in the drawer where he'd found it.

Professor Lamb threw up his hands. "Why take them if you were planning to return them?"

"I wasn't," Ollie admitted. "I intended to sell them to the highest bidder . . ."

"The man who bought you lobster and champagne at the Grand Hotel Majestic?" asked Harper.

He started guiltily. "How did you know?"

"The same one you were arguing with on the High Street yesterday?" said Kat.

Ollie's cheeks had taken on the hue of an overcooked beet. "Yes. I'm embarrassed to admit that he's a bone trader. I know you all hate me now, but there are reasons for what I did. I grew up dirt-poor—"

"So did I," snapped Jamal, "but I didn't turn to thieving to get out of it."

Ollie pressed on. "It's always been my dream to be a paleontologist. I was really proud to be the first in my family to go to university, but right from the start, I struggled to manage. Soon, I was up to my ears in debt. Then I learned about the Bone Wars."

"Did you say 'Bone Wars'?" asked Amy.

"Yup, otherwise known as the Great Dinosaur Rush. A hundred and fifty years ago, vast beds of dinosaur bones were discovered in the American West. Two rival paleontologists each dispatched teams to hunt down and claim as many dinosaurs as possible for cash and glory. The resulting ferocious feud—involving sabotage, bribery, bodily harm and, well . . . theft—became the stuff of legend. Ultimately, it ruined them both."

Harper and Kat exchanged glances, wondering again if Johnny Roswell had been murdered by a jealous fossil collector.

"I don't understand what the Bone Wars have to do with your stealing our Jurassic Dragon's teeth, Ollie," said Samira.

All eyes were on the squirming student, and nobody apart from Kat noticed one of the other volunteers sneaking into the passage.

Kat followed a minute later.

"Reading about the Bone Wars gave me the notion to use fossils to solve my own money problems," Ollie continued. "I'd found a trunkful of unidentified fossils in the university archives. I nicked one and sold it on a bone-collector website. It was easy, and I got away with it. So I did it again. And again. When Professor Lamb and I discovered the Jurassic Dragon, I was contacted by an ex-customer offering me enough cash to pay off my student loan. All he needed was the *long chi*—the dragon teeth. The temptation was too much to resist."

"Then why bring them back?" asked Professor Lamb.

"Because once I had them, all I could think about was how good you'd been to me and how much you'd trusted me, even though I didn't deserve it. I'm so sorry, sir. I'll get my belongings and leave now. The career I love is over, and I've no one to blame but myself."

"I won't hear of you quitting," said Theo Lamb. "If you promise to let this be a lesson learned, Oliver, I'll keep you on. You're clever, passionate, and hardworking, and you'll make a fine paleontologist one day."

When the rest of the crew protested, he hushed them. "Have you forgotten that Ollie returned the dracoraptor's teeth, and yet they're still missing? Will the real thief step forward?"

No one moved. Harper played the CCTV footage again. This time they watched as Jennifer—a volunteer who was later discovered to have given Bash a cupcake that upset his tummy—let herself in through the front door of the hall using a key she'd had cut. Then she brazenly hurried into the night with the pouch that Ollie had returned less than an hour before.

The rest of the team gasped and looked around, searching for her.

"Jennifer's gone," said Kat from the doorway. "I saw her nip to the bathroom while you were all yelling at Ollie. She picked up her jacket and crept out as if she was hoping no one would notice, which made me suspicious. Like maybe she had a guilty conscience about something. When she didn't come back, I ran to look for her, but she'd used the bathroom window as an escape route. She must have had a car waiting. I heard an engine."

As Professor Lamb and his crew tried to come to terms with the realization that the thief was their trusted friend and colleague, Kat and Harper were looking at the photo of Jennifer, still pinned on the bulletin board. She was grinning on the beach, holding a palmful of seashells. They'd been secretly hoping that when they did come across a member of the Order of Dragons, they'd look like a dinosaur-trading villain and not like Jennifer, who was bubbly, spoke with a posh accent, and looked like everyone's favorite sister, best friend, or niece.

If Jennifer was a Dragon, *anyone* could be a Dragon.

"Three break-ins in one night," marveled Harper after Professor Lamb had sent the crew out for breakfast. "That must be some kind of record. What will happen to Jennifer, Dad?"

"I suspect she's given me false contact details, so

probably nothing," replied her father, who was whistling as he washed up the coffee cups. "I'll give the police what I have, but I doubt they'll track her down."

"Then why are you so cheerful?" demanded Harper. "Aren't you upset that the dracoraptor's teeth are gone and will be sold on the black market?"

He dried his hands. "No, because they're not. I asked a model maker I know to create some realistic copies of them for me. Then I substituted them for the ones in the pouch. The real *long chi* are in the last place anyone would ever think of looking. I'll put the word out that an unidentified thief is still at large. Hopefully, the bone thieves will be too busy chasing after the fake teeth to bother with me and my team."

Later, Harper and Kat walked down to the harbor for an emergency Wolfe & Lamb Incorporated conference. They'd texted Edith to ask her to join them.

"The best thing about my dad and your mom is that they're optimists," Harper said to Kat as they strolled past the windsurfers and speedboats toward the end of the jetty. "They're always looking on the bright side of life and seeing the good in people. But that can be a problem too."

"Lucky we have Edith to balance things out, then," agreed Kat, as their librarian friend rattled across the boards on her mobility scooter.

"I was about to call you when I got your text," said

Edith, braking sharply. "I've found something that might be relevant—even more so, perhaps, now that the Jurassic Dragon's teeth have been stolen. Ever since I sent you the rejection letter Harry received from the editor of *Fossils Forever*, I've been searching for information on the Order of Dragons. They're elusive, to put it mildly. Finally, last night, I stumbled across a note about them in a self-published biography of Mary Anning."

She took the book from her basket. "Harper, your eyes are better than mine. Read this passage for me, will you?"

Harper flicked over the pages and then started to read aloud:

"The great English fossil hunter Mary Anning survived a landslide and was known for her fearlessness. Yet even she was said to have been unnerved by the ruthless antics of the Order of Dragons. Once common grave robbers turning bones into snake oil, the secretive nineteenth-century cult found fortune and infamy when its members began trading "dragon"-bone (dinosaur-fossil) tonics and tinctures as cures for everything from depression to brain tumors. Members of the Order of Dragons were rumored to be among the most illustrious figures in the land—politicians, academics, writers, and musicians. Some claim that the sect still exists today and has the same goal: immortality."

"*Immortality?*" repeated Kat. "You'd think they'd have figured out that their tonics didn't work when their members kept dying of old age. Nobody sane believes that potions made from dinosaur teeth will help them live forever."

"I disagree," said Edith. "A great many people would pay a lot for the chance to prolong life, especially if they're gravely ill. For the rich and powerful, health is the only thing money can't buy. If my arthritis gets any worse, I might be tempted to try a dragon tonic myself. Joke!" she said, seeing Harper's horrified face. "That was a joke, I promise."

Harper stared across the water at the old hall, thinking hard. What would happen when the bone collectors discovered they'd been cheated and had paid the earth for fiberglass teeth? They'd be back, she was sure of it, only this time they'd be wanting revenge. What would happen to her father and his young team then?

RUNAWAY

THERE ARE NO RECORDED CASES OF pythons demonstrating any gratitude toward their handlers, but it seemed to Kat that her absence had made Mr. Bojangles's cold heart grow fonder. For two whole days, he'd been on his best behavior. At no time had he attempted to crush her, escape, or dine on any small creatures, fresh or frozen.

While holding him, she was careful to keep him below her shoulders. As her mum had once warned, pythons couldn't be expected to distinguish between a neck and a vine, and a few seconds of pressure on a windpipe was all it would take to cause a person to black out.

As Kat refilled Mr. B's water bowl, Mario Rossi's sound system lit up. A digital voice said blandly, "Message for Ninety-Nine. Spots spotted. Repeat: Spots spotted.

Immediate action required. SY 83412 79954. Repeat: SY 83412 79954. Over and out."

Cycling home, Kat wondered what it could mean. She hadn't managed to jot down the numbers, but she did recall the first part, SY 834, and the spotted spots. Did everyone speak in code these days? She was more certain than ever that Mario and Mr. B were in Bluebell Bay for something that had nothing whatsoever to do with coasteering.

Immediate action required, the message had said. *What* action? Her grandfather had told her that these days, spies where everywhere. Was Mario in town spying on a restaurant rival, or had he used the camouflage kayak in the photo to blow up the cliff so he could sell fossils to a bone collector too?

First chance she got, she planned to ask him about the kayak. It would be interesting to see what he had to say.

Mario was forgotten the minute Kat reached her own home and saw that her bedroom window was open! Three times, her mum had reminded her to tell the cleaner who came once a week to stay out of her room in case Tiny escaped. Three times, Kat had managed to forget.

She tore up to the attic, but it was too late. Tiny was missing.

Kat collapsed onto her bed in despair. If Tiny had been snatched and was on his way to Mr. Bludger's animal prison, she'd have no one to blame but herself.

Then she sat up again. There was no time for self-pity. Her mum and Tina had a full caseload. They'd be at the clinic for another three hours at least. Kat couldn't wait till then. If Mr. Bludger was lurking in the neighborhood with his trap, every minute mattered.

Kat washed her face and went across to the animal clinic. Her best hope of finding Tiny fast was to take Pax with her to sniff out the Savannah.

As a precaution, she took the Pi-Craft pen out of the army briefcase she kept concealed behind a bookcase. She'd examined it and found it was indeed a digital voice recorder. If she ran into the animal control officer, it would do no harm at all to record their conversation. Mr. Bludger was a bully, and Kat knew bullies have a habit of being extra mean if they thought there were no witnesses around.

The animal clinic reception room was packed. Nurse Tina had barely a second to smile and say, "Come to take Pax for a wander? She'll be ecstatic to see you."

She was. After Kat had been thoroughly appreciated, she hoisted a cat carrier rucksack over her shoulders and put a leash on the collie. They left via the rear door of the kennels. Half of Bluebell Bay knew that Tiny was a wanted cat, suspected of sheep worrying. The last thing Kat needed was anyone to witness her searching for him in the fields around Wiley Evans's farm.

Pax's paw was healing beautifully. Her limp was hardly noticeable as she followed Kat up the wooded slope behind the practice. Kat tried to imagine which way she'd walk if she were a cat. At the back of her mind was the vague hope that if a rogue creature was killing sheep, Pax might flush them out.

Almost immediately, the collie picked up a thrilling scent. Kat had to jog to keep up with her. They crossed a field and a stream lined with willow trees. As they scrambled up a shaded bank, Pax began barking wildly. A man was scanning the farm buildings with binoculars. He had his back to them, but Kat recognized him before he swung round. He did not look pleased to see her. At all.

"What are *you* doing here?"

"Hi, Mario. Quiet, Pax. Sit. Good girl." Kat hoped Mario Rossi wouldn't look too closely at the cat carrier. "I'm just walking my dog. What are you up to?"

"Only fishing."

He held up a wire basket. Kat made out a dull-eyed carp through the mesh. It smelled at least twenty-four-hours old. That was suspicious, but not nearly as fishy as the red mud that was caked on his boots or the rifle-shaped case slung over his shoulder. Had Pax not been at her side and bristling, Kat would have been worried.

What was Mario doing with what she was sure was

a gun? Was he out hunting pheasant or deer? Her gaze went to the binoculars.

"Bird-watching," he told her before she could ask. "Great seeing you, Kat. I must be going. Thanks again for taking care of Mr. B. He's a rescue and can be tricky, so you're obviously a brilliant pet sitter." Vaulting over a low fence, he was gone.

Kat shivered. His compliments meant nothing to her. He was lying about the fishing. She'd have to be careful. If he found out that she'd heard the radio message addressing him or someone else on the same radio frequency as "Ninety-Nine" before passing on a coded message, things could get ugly.

Infuriatingly, she'd put herself in jeopardy for no purpose. She'd been silly to think she could find Tiny out in the woods and fields. It would have been far better to wait for him at home. He was probably there now, meowing for treats. Kat suddenly felt despairing. "Come on, Pax. Let's get home."

Right then, a van came roaring along the nearby lane. Over the top of the hedgerow, Kat saw the animal control van speed by on its way to the farm.

What if Bludger was after Tiny? She began to run.

Pax needed no encouragement to head for the farmyard. When she reached the gate, Kat crouched behind a thicket of brambles and put her hand over the collie's muzzle. Mr. Bludger was talking to the farmer's wife. She pointed toward a barn inside a pasture full of sheep.

Mr. Bludger lifted the trap from his van, and Kat's heart almost stopped. Her Way of the Mongoose rehearsals now seemed ridiculous. What was she going to do—run into the yard and attempt to stop the animal control officer with a Butterfly Sweep?

But just then the farmer's wife gestured toward the farmhouse, perhaps to invite Mr. Bludger in for tea. Rubbing his considerable stomach, he followed her inside.

Kat tied the collie to the fence. "Stay, Pax. I won't be long. Stay!"

Skipping across a cattle guard, she sprinted to the barn. She was almost there when she heard barking.

Pax had slipped her leash and was in among the sheep, trying to herd them into a corner. The farmer's wife dashed from the house. Mr. Bludger emerged behind her, snatched up his trap, and came in lumbering pursuit.

Kat darted into the barn. While they were distracted by Pax, there might still be time to save Tiny—if he was there. But as she paused to allow her eyes to adjust to the gloom, a blood-freezing snarl cut through the shadows.

"Tiny?" Kat said nervously. "Tiny, don't be afraid. It's me. I've come to take you home."

Instinct made her glance up. Four green eyes stared

down at her from a wooden beam. Kat blinked. She must be seeing double, she thought.

It was her last thought before a blur of spots and stripes came at her. In mid-pounce, Kat recognized one cat as a lynx. The second was Tiny. He launched himself at the lynx, knocking it aside. They hit the ground together. The wildcat twisted upright and was gone with a hiss.

Kat knelt and hugged Tiny, who was winded but unharmed. "You saved me! Who *was* that? Where did it come from?"

To Tiny's horror, she bundled him into the carrier. "Sorry, baby, but we have to get out of here." But as she struggled to lift the cat carrier on to her back, the barn door was shoved aside. Behind the animal control officer, the farmer's wife had Pax by the collar.

"Well, whaddya know," crowed Mr. Bludger. "We've got ourselves two scoundrels for the price of one."

DRAGON BOY

Natural History Museum, London

"HARPER, ARE YOU *SURE* THIS IS A GOOD idea?" fretted Kat two days later as they outpaced Tina Chung in a bid to reach the Natural History Museum by 10:45 A.M.

They'd planned to arrive earlier, but their train from Wool to Waterloo had been delayed. "We absolutely can't be late," said Harper. "It's critical we're in position by eleven. Dragon Boy promised to wait five minutes and not a second more. We have to allow extra time in case anything goes wrong. Tina might want to browse the gift shop or linger over a cup of tea."

It was Thursday morning. If anyone had told Kat that forty-eight hours after her cat and dog had been dragged yowling and howling to the animal control prison she'd be on her way to London to meet a stranger who called himself "Dragon Boy," she'd have declared them stark raving crazy. And yet here she was.

Weirder still, she'd been inspired to come by Robyn. That was the name of the homeless woman. Kat had bumped into her the day after Mr. Bludger had wrenched Tiny from her grasp. Given a choice, she'd have spent the rest of her life under her duvet, but she had pet-sitting commitments. It wasn't the python or horses' fault that her own animals had been dragged away like criminals.

As Kat pedaled miserably from one end of Bluebell Bay to the other, Robyn had stepped into her path. "I heard what happened to your animals. I'm so sorry," she'd said, before pressing a scroll of brown paper into Kat's palm. It was secured with a ribbon of bark threaded with sprigs of lavender.

Kat had barely had time to thank her or ask her name before Robyn—"with a *y*"—was halfway across a field, sleeping bag slung over her shoulder.

Kat had waited until she was back at Summer Street to open the scroll. Inside was an exquisite ink sketch of Winnie the Pooh with a cloud of bees around his bear ears:

Always remember . . .
you are braver than you believe,
stronger than you seem,
and smarter than you think.

The thoughtfulness of the gift and the power of the words had lifted Kat's spirits like nothing else. By the time Harper had rung with a convoluted tale about meeting "Dragon Boy" in an online fossil forum, Kat was not only willing to go along with Harper's grand scheme, she'd helped talk Tina into taking them to London's Natural History Museum on her day off.

But Kat hadn't agreed to anything until she'd grilled Harper on how and where she'd found this boy who claimed to have information on the Order of Dragons. "How do you know he's not a sixty-year-old ax murderer pretending to be a kid?"

"Because I told him to meet us at eleven on the bench beneath the blue whale skeleton, and he said he'd buffer there for five minutes max. How many adults do you know who'd say *buffer* instead of *wait*?"

"That's it? That's your only proof?"

"Are you kidding? Dad would kill me if 'safety first' wasn't my online motto. So would Jasper. He checked him out for me. Dragon Boy's good at hiding his IP address, but not as good as he thinks he is. We're ninety-nine point nine percent sure that he's a twelve-year-old gaming fanatic. Pretty talented at it too."

"How's he going to assist us?" Kat wasn't clear about that part.

"He might not. We won't know till we meet him. All I did was visit a couple of fossil-collecting sites and drop a few hints that I was working on a Jurassic Coast excavation and would consider parting with a few dragon teeth in exchange for some information about the Order of Dragons."

Kat was horrified. "You don't own any dracoraptor teeth!"

"No, but I have a few pretend ones. Dad had a spare set made when he asked the sculptor to make the others. I borrowed them."

"What happens if this boy realizes they're pretend, and things turn nasty?"

But Harper just waved away her fears. "We'll be in the crowded main hall of the Natural History Museum. If he turns psycho on us, we'll scream blue murder, and Tina and half a dozen security guards and brave members of the public will come running. It'll be fine. What could possibly go wrong?"

"I don't understand why you're tearing along like cats with their tails on fire," said Tina once they entered the museum. "It was clearly a mistake to allow you to eat so much chocolate on the train. Harper almost hyperventilated when the subway got stuck in that tunnel. And now that we're finally here, you want to race from exhibit to exhibit."

"We only want to see as much as possible," said Kat.

They'd persuaded Tina to begin with the first floor,

where they'd have a bird's-eye view of the bench beneath the whale skeleton. They planned to watch from a safe distance until they were sure that Dragon Boy wasn't a potential kidnapper.

At eleven o'clock, a man wearing a black leather trench coat and dark sunglasses indoors—a Mafia hit man, if Kat ever saw one—took ownership of the bench. His menacing looks frightened away two pensioners.

"Seems like Dragon Boy might be Dragon *Man*," remarked Kat when Tina was out of earshot.

"Or Dragon Boy is as nervous as we are," said Harper. "Look over there."

Across the hall, a black-haired boy was leaning over the balustrade, gaze fixed on the assassin type on the bench. Below them, the man jumped up, his face relaxing into a grin as he was engulfed by an adoring wife and two children. *Not a hit man, then*, thought Kat, who was beginning to doubt her own judgment. She and Harper watched as the boy rushed down the steps and took the man's place on the bench.

"Game on," said Harper. "Tell Tina you have an overwhelming urge to visit the American mastodon—that's an Ice Age relative of the elephant. I'll say I need the bathroom and that I'll meet you on the bench. Meanwhile, I'll try to get some information out of Dragon Boy. If I scream, come to my rescue."

Everything went according to plan right up until Harper handed the boy the false dragon's teeth. They'd been sitting back-to-back on the bench, as if they had nothing to do with each other, talking out of the corners of their mouths.

"What do you know about the Order of Dragons?" was Harper's first question.

The boy stared around in a panic, as if a doom of dragons might swoop on them. "Never, ever say their name out loud," he said. "Call them the OD, in case anyone overhears. I'll tell you one thing, then you give me the *long chi*, and we go our separate ways."

Harper kept a wary eye on Tina and Kat over by the mastodon. "Make it short and sweet. I don't have much time."

"They're a dragon cult. They worship dragons. My family is Chinese. In our culture, dragons have a special significance. They symbolize power, wisdom, happiness, and immortality, and they bring prosperity. They have unlimited supernatural gifts. A dragon can transform itself into any shape, from a snake to a storm, and they can stop floods and tsunamis." He paused. "That's it, until you hand over the dragon's teeth."

Harper risked turning around. "You cannot be serious. You expect me to give you two *long chi* for some stuff straight out of a Terry Pratchett novel? At least tell me why the dragon's teeth are so important to the OD. What do they do with them?"

"They want to live forever."

"Seriously? Who believes that?"

He exhaled. "Okay, among some practitioners of Chinese alchemy, dragon's teeth are highly prized. One of the oldest texts on traditional Chinese medicine says *long chi* can be used to cure epilepsy, madness, and convulsions. My father has a dictionary of Chinese medicine that lists "dragon's bone and teeth" as a tranquilizer. It claims that *long chi* can be used as a sedative to treat insomnia, depression, fever, and liver disease, among other things. And some people take it to an extreme. They believe dragon energy has the power to extend life. That's why the OD wants it. They want to live forever. Now give me the dragon's teeth."

Reluctantly, Harper handed over a velvet pouch. She felt guilty about giving him fake fossils. He seemed vulnerable, as if he was in some kind of trouble. "How do you know about the OD?" she asked. "Have you met any of them?"

He tipped the fossils into his palm and sniffed them. The blood drained from his face. He began to shake.

Harper was alarmed. "What's wrong? Are you ill?"

"You tricked me," he said in a low, exhausted voice. "These are fakes. You were my last hope. We're dead now, me and my dad. That's what they've told us. If Patient X dies, they'll kill us."

Harper knew in that instant that, whatever she and Kat had stumbled upon, it was no longer a game. "Who are *they*? And who is Patient X?"

"There you are, Harper!" cried Tina, interrupting. "You wouldn't believe how obsessed Kat is with the mastodon. I couldn't drag her away."

Harper mustered her most cheerful voice. "Tina, would you mind if we visited the main dinosaur exhibition now? I'd love to show you both the megalosaurus tooth."

The boy was ready to make a run for it, but she gripped his sleeve as Kat distracted Tina.

"If you're in trouble, me and my friend can help you," Harper told him. "That's what we do."

"I doubt it," he said bitterly.

"Never, ever underestimate girls," Harper cautioned him. "Especially not girl detectives."

He turned on her. "Listen, Nancy Drew, Sherlock Holmes himself couldn't help us. You can't fathom who we're up against. These people are monsters."

Neurons sparked in Harper's brain, lighting up connections. All along, she and Kat had been working on the theory that a valuable fossil or an investigation into some nature-destroying company had gotten Johnny killed. They hadn't considered that he might have delved into the murky, cutthroat world of the illegal bone traders.

"Are the OD monstrous enough to kill a young reporter who might have been investigating them?" she said urgently. "Because that's the case my best friend and I are working on now. After a landslide in our town, a human skeleton was discovered. We believe that the victim, Johnny Roswell, was murdered. Me and Kat— that's her over there in the dolphin T-shirt—also have a hunch that bone collectors are linked to a break-in at the hall where my father's working. Dad's a paleontologist."

The boy leaped off the bench as if it had suddenly become red-hot. "You never said on the forum that your dad was a paleontologist! What are you doing here? Is this a trap?"

"Harper, why are you dragging your feet?" called Tina. "I thought you wanted to show us the megalosaurus tooth."

Under cover of tying her shoelaces, Harper hissed to the boy, "You never said you were in danger on the forum either. And, no, this isn't a trap. Tell us what you know. If the OD is blackmailing you, we can help—even if it's only online. Follow us to the dinosaur hall. We'll talk between exhibits." She raised her voice. "Coming, Tina! I had a stone in my sneaker."

In the dinosaur hall, she and Kat took turns conducting their most surreal client interview ever. While Harper told Tina everything she never wanted to know about the torvosaurus claw, Kat dropped back to listen to the boy's story. His name was Kai. In November, nearly eight months earlier, a stranger had walked into Eastern Healing, his father's acupuncture and traditional medicine practice, and blackmailed Dr. Liu into making a dinosaur tincture for a grievously ill person known only as Patient X. Since then, their lives had been a daily nightmare.

"If your father doesn't deal in illegal fossils, where did he get the *long chi* he gave the patient?" accused Kat.

"A long time ago, a trader tried to sell him rare Maotianshan fossils from Chengjiang in China. Dad was refusing them when the police raided, looking for rhino horn. The trader dropped the fossils and ran. Dad hid them, thinking he'd come back for them, but he never did."

Kat must have looked disbelieving because Kai said angrily, "My father is one of the best doctors in the U.K. He's never used fossils in his life and thinks it's a crime that unscrupulous bone collectors are destroying paleontology sites across China and in other countries. It made him ill to grind up the rare fossils for the stranger. He did his best to warn the man that the *long chi* wouldn't cure the patient because the medical records show they have a terminal condition."

Kat's heart skipped a beat. "Are you saying that Patient X is *dying*? Dr. Liu's sure of that?"

"One hundred percent. The patient has a rare

cancer. It spreads slowly, but there is no cure. When the man from the OD refused to take no for an answer, Dad hoped that the dragon's teeth would have what doctors call a "placebo effect." If a patient believes strongly enough that a pill or potion is working, it can temporarily improve their symptoms or take away their pain. Dad and I badly wanted the stories about the *long chi*'s powers of healing to be true. We needed a miracle."

"Did you get it?"

"For a while, yes. Then last week, the same man called in a rage to say the patient was getting worse. In three days, our *long chi* will run out. Dad and I are afraid for our lives."

"Kat, come and look at this interesting exhibit on the dragon doctors of ancient China," called Tina. "Dinosaur remains were believed to be those of dead dragons and were ground up for medicine."

Kat lifted an eyebrow at Kai, then got up to join Tina. While she and the nurse enthused over dragon doctors, Harper slipped back to talk to Kai.

"How did you work out the Order—I mean, the OD—were the ones blackmailing you?"

"Every month, an envelope arrives in the post. No postmark. Inside is a map of Hyde Park with an *X* on it. I drop the medicine in the nearest trash can. I've never seen anyone collect it. Last month, I had the idea of rubbing the back of the map with charcoal in case someone had leaned on it to write something—a phone number, a name. Anything. This came up."

He showed her a photo on his phone. Harper gasped. It was a dragon with its tail twisted into an infinity symbol—identical to the one on the black-and-gold card Kat had lost. Only Kai's dragon had a scroll above its head: "ORDER OF DRAGONS: *In aeternum vive*." To live forever.

The boy was watching her. "You've seen it before? Where?"

"On a card someone dropped at a hotel in Bluebell Bay."

Tina glanced around, searching for Harper. Kai shot behind a glass cabinet. He said hurriedly, "After I found the dragon image, I asked around my friends. Kept it cool. One boy recognized it right away as the sign of the OD. His father told him it was a secret club, like the Masons, for rich, ruthless people who don't want to die. They pay the highest prices for the best fossils with the strongest dragon energy, but my friend's dad said their money wasn't worth it because bad things happen to traders who deal with them."

Tina started toward Harper, but Kat diverted her to a chart on the death of the dinosaurs. They were nearly at the end of the exhibition. Time was running out.

Harper said quickly, "Kai, can you describe the stranger who came to your father's practice?"

"He was very tall. Not much else, because he wore a mask and gloves. His coat looked expensive. A posh English accent. I got the feeling he was someone important, so maybe Patient X is someone high up in the OD—otherwise, why would he bother? I do remember one silly thing. He was wearing these smart black shoes with blue laces."

Harper's heart rate spiked. "Navy blue or sky blue?"

"Sky blue. I thought I'd be able trace where they were made. I was hoping they would be very rare. Then I find they're in fashion. There are trillions of them."

Harper nodded. She'd come to the same conclusion. "Kai, last weekend, we were at Kat's grandfather's house. He's the minister of defense."

Kai stared at her. "Who *are* you people?"

"Doesn't matter. While we were there, I overheard a weird conversation. I couldn't see the men talking, only that one of them was wearing blue laces. Blue-Lace Man was ranting about a father and son—'business associates,' he called them—and saying that when they'd outlived their usefulness, they'd . . ."

Harper's voice trailed off. She could hardly tell Kai that the man had discussed eliminating him and his dad.

Kai filled in the blanks. "Disappear? Be killed?"

Harper didn't answer. "He seemed to think that the boy could see through his scheming—see right into his soul. The other man was teasing him about dusting cobwebs off it."

"Could have been talking about anyone," said Kai, "but it is quite a coincidence. What's his name?"

"We're still trying to find out. He and his friend were talking in riddles about an order. The second guy wanted to buy two black T-shirts for his arthritis and a striped one because his wife was redecorating. He also asked for a fancy white plastic—" She stopped when she saw Kai's face. "What have I said? What's wrong?"

"That's black-market code for illegal wildlife products. Dad and I love all animals, and my father's spent most of his life fighting the illegal trade. *Two black T-shirts* equals two ounces of powdered rhino horn. *Striped T-shirts* are tiger skins. *White plastic*, that's ivory. *Red plastic* is pangolin scales . . ."

"Harper, I'm really surprised at you," scolded Tina, popping up out of nowhere and forcing Kai to dive under a display to avoid detection. "Kat told me you were desperate to visit the Natural History Museum for a school project. But every time I've glanced around, you've either been missing or staring into space. What's going on? Are you unwell?"

While Harper spouted nonsense about how being close to the triceratops skull had put her into a dreamy state of wonder, Kat met Kai under the table. "Any clues that might help us identify Patient X? Age? Gender? Symptoms?"

"No, because the personal details had been blacked out on the medical forms. There is one thing though. This cancer, it attacks the liver. The whites of the patient's eyes turn yellow, like mustard. There's cosmetic stuff they can do to hide it in the early stages, but it won't last long."

"KAT WOLFE, what are you up to?" Tina reached down and pulled Kat up by the hand. "I'm not sure what mischief you and Harper are plotting, but I'm not having it. Fun is canceled for the rest of the day. We're taking the next train back to Dorset. You can eat sandwiches from the buffet car on the way."

There was no chance to say goodbye to Kai, although Harper did manage to scribble her number on a ticket stub and toss it to him. As they exited the museum, she could think of nothing but the threat she'd overheard at Hamilton Park: *When the boy and his dad have outlived their usefulness, they'll be eliminated.*

If Wolfe & Lamb didn't crack the case soon, Kai and Dr. Liu would be as extinct as the museum's blue whale. And if the Order of Dragons was responsible for Johnny's death, it would mean they'd be getting away with murder again.

WILDCATS

FROM THE MOMENT SHE'D LAID EYES ON IT, Kat had adored her attic room. Its sea views, futon bed, and crowded bookshelves were a dream come true. But with Tiny gone, it felt cold and full of ghosts. She pined for his warmth, his wildcat energy, and even his moods. They changed like the weather, and Kat enjoyed the challenge of responding to them. Few things were more rewarding than comforting him if he was distressed by thunder or the neighbor's lawn mower and hearing his purr swell in his chest.

Who would comfort him now? Was there a single kind person in charge of the confiscated creatures in the animal control center? Did Tiny and Pax have blankets and fresh water in their grim concrete cells?

As Kat wiped away tears, she suddenly recalled her grandfather telling her he'd be there for her if she was ever in trouble. Before he became minister of defense, he'd been a lawyer. Perhaps he could call heartless Mr. Bludger and inform him that animals, like people, were innocent until proven guilty.

His mobile phone went straight to voicemail, so she tried Hamilton Park. Freya answered on the first ring.

"Kat? What a lovely surprise. His Lordship will be sorry to have missed you. He's out of the country, but I'll tell him you called when he's back. Can I pass on a message?"

"What about V?" Kat asked on impulse. "Is he there?"

There was a pause. "Who's V?"

"Never mind," Kat said quickly. "Freya, I know it's an odd question, but have you noticed anyone at Hamilton Park wearing blue shoelaces?"

The PA laughed. "I've heard some funny questions in my time, but that tops them all. Why do you want to know?"

Kat decided that honesty was the policy most likely to get results. "When we were staying with you, Harper heard two people discussing buying striped T-shirts and white plastic carvings. We've just found out that some criminals use that as code for buying illegal tiger skins and ivory. So, you see, it's quite important."

"I hope to goodness you're mistaken," Freya said worriedly. "His Lordship would go berserk if he thought that those sorts of conversations were taking place under his roof. As you know, he's obsessed with saving wildlife. Let me think. Sheila in accounts has sneakers in every color of the rainbow, but she has ten cats so I doubt—"

"They were men," Kat interrupted.

"Hmm. In PR, Jay Read has taken to wearing purple laces with his brogues. Even the Grim Reaper—that's my nickname for one of the civil servants in the Ministry of the Environment—has an attachment to colored laces. Are they blue or are they orange? I can't remember, to be honest. I remember thinking it surprising because he's the dullest man in existence. Sir Haslemere was in gold laces last time he visited. He's in hospital, you know. Rushed in for an emergency op last night. Now him I *can* imagine buying tiger skins and ivory, but then maybe I'm biased. In any case, I will let you know if I spot any blue laces at Hamilton Park."

"Kat, I have to show you this!" cried her mum, rushing into the room. She stopped when she saw that Kat was on a call.

"Thanks, Freya—just tell my grandfather I rang," said Kat, and switched off her phone.

Her mum smiled. "Keeping in touch with your grandfather?"

"Trying to," said Kat. "He's abroad."

Her mum sat down beside her. "I wanted to show you this. It's a plaster cast of the pawprint of an endangered Iberian lynx."

Kat ran her fingers over the hollows in the smooth plaster, imagining the leathery pads and razor claws of the wildcat. "Where did you get it?"

"Last weekend, I found a partial pawprint at Wiley Evans's farm. A university friend who specializes in wildcats has just confirmed its species. I haven't said anything until now because I didn't want to get your hopes up."

"An *Iberian* lynx is on the loose in Bluebell Bay?" said Kat excitedly, feeling a pang of guilt that she hadn't told her mum about the wildcat she'd seen when she was out searching for Tiny. Nor had she mentioned seeing Mario Rossi near the farm, with a rifle-shaped bag. Had she known the lynx was endangered, she'd have alerted her mother right away. "*That's* what's been attacking the sheep? Where could it have escaped from?"

"A zoo or maybe a private collector. If it was being kept illegally, they might not have wanted to tell the police it had run off in case they were prosecuted."

"But even if it's never found, this pawprint cast proves that Tiny and Pax are innocent, doesn't it, Mum? Mr. Bludger will *have* to believe us now."

"Sadly, nothing but an actual living, breathing lynx will convince that miserable man to release our cat and collie. We need physical proof."

"Then we'll just have to get it." Kat expected her mum to demur.

Instead, Dr. Wolfe said, "Yes, and we'll need to

move fast. Whoever stole or lost the lynx is most probably hunting for it and could return, armed, at any time. They're unlikely to want to part with their valuable cat, so we'll need to tread carefully. Let's leave at twilight. Dress in black."

The relief Kat felt at having her mum take charge was quite overwhelming. She wished she'd remembered that where animals were concerned, her mum was always in her corner.

"Good thing I spotted that paragraph in today's *Bluebell Bay Gazette* about a motorist claiming to have seen an enormous spotted cat near Chris Carmichael's farm," said Dr. Wolfe as they walked up a lane striped with swaying shadows. "We'll start here and go to Wiley's farm afterward if we have no luck."

An enormous spotted cat.

All at once, Kat knew exactly why Mario Rossi was in Bluebell Bay. She'd been so devastated about her pets being dragged away by Mr. Bludger that she'd failed to make the connection between the *spots spotted* message she'd heard in Mario's motor home and the spotted cat that had sprung at her. The numbers in the message must have been map coordinates! *That's* why Mario had been studying the farm outbuildings with binoculars and why he'd been so irritated to see her. He'd been hunting the lynx.

Everything made sense if he was a wildlife trafficker. Was he part of a gang stealing and selling endangered animals—alive or dead—to the Far East? Was Mr. Bojangles stolen too?

"Mum . . . ," she began as they reached the gates of the farm.

But Dr. Wolfe held up a hand. "Sorry, Kat—I thought I heard something. Are you okay to wait by the barn? Don't go inside. I'll need to ask Chris Carmichael's permission to search it. It might be simpler if I do that on my own."

As Kat neared the barn, she thought she heard a growl. Worried that the lynx might get away again, leaving Tiny and Pax locked up forever, she stepped through the dark doorway. The air was heavy with the sweet smell of hay—and something else. Something wild. The hairs stood up on the back of Kat's neck. The lynx was there; she sensed it. Before she could retreat and wait for her mum, a silhouette sharpened into focus. A man was aiming a high-powered rifle at her. There was a silencer on it. Her mum wouldn't hear a thing.

"Don't move," Mario said softly. "Don't even breathe."

Then he fired.

The bullet passed so close to Kat's cheek that she felt it scorch by like a mini comet. She barely had time to take in that she was still alive when the lynx thudded into the straw at her feet. It lay motionless, eyes empty. Kat screamed and screamed.

Dr. Wolfe burst in, taking in Kat's terrified face, the lynx on the ground, and Mario Rossi's smoking gun. After rushing to give her daughter a consoling hug, she smiled at the Italian. "If you're who I think you are— boy, am I glad to see you."

Kat gaped as Mario stepped forward to shake her mum's hand. "Dr. Wolfe, I presume? I'm Mario Rossi. Apologies. I think I gave Kat an awful scare."

The vet bent down to check the lynx's pulse, saying over her shoulder: "Kat, honey, I know it's a shock to see her lying so still, but she'll recover beautifully. Mr. Rossi used a tranquilizer dart. She's only sleeping." She stood up. "Wait a second, Mr. Rossi just called you Kat. Do you two know each other?"

Kat found her voice at last. "I do a bit of pet sitting for Mario. I saw him near Wiley's farm yesterday and was afraid he might be a hunter."

Her mum laughed. "He's the opposite of a hunter. In conservation circles, Mario Rossi's a legend. He's one of the finest wildlife crime detectives in the world."

Kat was impressed but bewildered. If Mario was such a hero, what had he been doing with the camouflage kayak? Was that a coincidence too?

Mario had gone red. "Your mum is very kind, Kat,

but, like the two of you, I'm only doing what I can to save animals. Sorry I couldn't be more truthful with you about my reasons for visiting Bluebell Bay. Two weeks ago, an endangered lynx was reported stolen from a Devon zoo. There was nothing on CCTV, and the zoo claimed they'd lost its paperwork, so police suspected an insurance scam or that they were selling animals to wildlife traffickers to raise cash. A couple of days later, a van with traces of lynx fur and blood in the back was found abandoned not far from Bluebell Bay. I was dispatched immediately to try to track her down. The Jurassic Dragon crowds complicated matters. If news that a wildcat had escaped here had gone viral, it would have caused mass panic. Added to which, trigger-happy farmers, hunters, and poachers would have descended upon your pretty town. I had to do the whole thing on the quiet."

Dr. Wolfe put her jacket over the lynx's tawny body. "With your permission, Mario, I'd like to get her to my clinic as fast as possible to give her some fluids and a thorough health check before you move her. I presume you have a safe place in mind?"

"Yes, we do. Thanks, Dr. Wolfe. I'd appreciate any help you can give her." He glanced at Kat. "Could I respectfully ask you both to keep her capture between us?"

"Mum, what about Tiny and Pax?" Kat said fearfully.

"If we can't say that a lynx was responsible for the sheep worrying, how will we free them from animal control?"

"I heard about an animal control officer snatching a cat and dog from a child. If they were yours, Kat, I'm very sorry—especially since you've been so wonderful with Mr. B. Leave it to me. I'll talk to the farmers. When I'm done presenting them each with compensation for the loss of their sheep, they'll be delighted to tell Mr. Bludger that it was all a bad dream."

SNAKE OIL

KAT BRUSHED ORKAAN UNTIL HER COAT shone like silk and planted a kiss on her velvety black muzzle. It was Friday afternoon, nine days since the Swanns had arrived in Bluebell Bay. The actor hadn't come to ride the mare once.

"If he doesn't show up tomorrow, I'm taking you to the beach, and we'll race along the edge of the waves," Kat told her. "It's not fair of Ethan to expect you to be cooped up here while he's out enjoying himself. Every horse needs to feel the wind in its mane."

Up at the house, she found Harper flipping through *Nature World* with Bailey on her shoulder. "Edith came by with these. Remember how Harry Holt ruined the library copy of *The Sixth Extinction* and left her *The Hobbit* and a bunch of old magazines as compensation? Turns out the magazines are packed with Johnny's stories. I wonder if Harry actually gave them to Edith for safekeeping—in case something happened to him."

Kat helped herself to a coconut macaroon. "Wouldn't they be online?"

"Yes, but before his arrest, Harry had become a virtual hermit. Maybe he didn't have the internet or even a computer. What if Johnny hid clues about the story he was investigating in among his cute tips on insect hotels? Clues that only he and Harry could understand."

"A secret code, you mean?"

"Uh-huh. Although I've tried a few of the most common, and nothing's worked so far. There's nth letter code, where every tenth letter, say, spells out *SOS*. Or acrostic, where the message is in the first letter of every word. You can also switch letters of the alphabet so *Q* means *A*. But even easy codes can take forever to figure out."

Kat opened her notebook. "Let's take another look at our mini mysteries. Maybe this time, we'll see a connection."

She found the page on which she'd drawn a ring of balloons, each containing a mystery. Now she drew two new balloons, labeling them: "*The Mystery of the Man in the Blue Laces*" and "*The Mystery of Patient X*." After a moment, she added another: "*The Bluefin Tuna Mystery*."

An electric tingle ran through her.

"What?" cried Harper, seeing her face. "What is it?"

"I've been a class-A dunce, that's what."

"Why? What have you seen? *Tell me!*"

"The connection—it's been staring us in the face all along."

"I don't understand," said Harper. "What does Blue-Shoelace Man have in common with bluefin tuna, apart from the color . . . ? Oh, wait. Make that two class-A dunces. The answer's so obvious, I'm going to write it in your notebook with a pink neon marker."

And she did.

EXTINCTION

Kat began pacing around the model dinosaur. "Ten of our thirteen mini mysteries are linked to extinction. Eleven if you count the Mystery of the Stolen Iberian Lynx. We know that the Order of Dragons has been buying rare fossils for centuries, and that the dragon key card we found is their symbol. Kai's sure that they're the ones blackmailing Dr. Liu into making dragon's teeth potions for Patient X. And we're sure that whoever blew up the cliff did it to uncover the Jurassic Dragon or other fossils, and that Ollie and the thief who tried to steal the *long chi* were trading dinosaur bones on the black market. Every one of those things is about extinct creatures."

Harper said excitedly, "Plus, the man with blue laces

was taking orders for rhino horn and tiger skin—from animals that'll soon be extinct in the wild. If only we could identify him, it might unlock another piece of the puzzle. Any word from your grandfather?"

"He texted last night to say he'd ring when—" Kat stopped midsentence as her gaze fell on Johnny's fox story. "You know that saying about not letting foxes guard henhouses?"

"Uh . . . no? Why, because they'd eat the chickens?"

"No. I mean, yes—but I don't mean real foxes. If you wanted to buy or sell endangered animal products, and you also happened to work for the government, where would you try to get a job?"

Harper let out a squeak of horror. "The Ministry of the Environment! Surely no one would be that . . . calculating?"

"But what if they were?" said Kat. "Working on the inside, they could make deals with poachers or help them get away with crimes, and get their hands on confiscated ivory or whatever. Freya thought she'd seen the man who works for the Ministry of the Environment wearing colored laces. She called him the Grim Reaper. Apparently, he's the dullest man in the universe, but that could be an act. Dull people don't get noticed. She couldn't remember his real name."

"On it," said Harper, opening her laptop and searching for Ministry of the Environment staff.

As soon as they saw his photo, they were sure they had the right man. Lucian Rigley, program manager for International Wildlife Outreach.

"Looks like the Grim Reaper," said Harper. "Looks like the type who'd want a tiger-skin rug in his library too."

"But is he also the type who'd be a member of a society that thinks dinosaur teeth can cure cancer?" asked Kat. "Is he capable of blackmail? Don't forget, we were wrong about Harry in the beginning."

"True, but gut instinct tells me we're on to something with Lucian Rigley," said Harper. "I do hope your grandfather calls soon. If Mr. Rigley *is* a snake-oil salesman who deals in rhino horn, he's capable of anything. But unless we can get some proof, he'll get away with it."

"We can't give up," said Kat. "We're so close. I can feel it."

"We'd better be," her friend said worriedly. "Kai's counting on us to save him and his dad before they're 'eliminated.'"

Kat's phone cheeped in the pocket of her breeches. She cheered when she read the message, tossing it onto the sofa before dancing around the room. "That was Mum. Tiny's coming ho-o-ome," she sang. "Pax is coming ho-o-ome!"

"That's fantastic news!" said Harper, laughing. "I'll

keep thinking about secret codes and foxes in henhouses. You go, go, go, Detective Wolfe!"

"Are you sure? They're not coming for hours, but I'd like to get their food and beds ready. Keep me posted, Detective Lamb. We'll solve the case—I know we will. My grandfather says that even dragons have their ending."

HOW TO BE BRAVE

AFTER KAT HAD GONE, HARPER REMEM-
bered where she'd seen that quote before. She found it in
Harry's copy of *The Hobbit*.

> So comes snow after fire, and even dragons have
> their ending.

It was the third time the book had come up in the
past week. Freya had mentioned that Sir Haslemere had
requested a first edition of *The Hobbit* when he came
to stay at Hamilton Park. If there was a secret code,
perhaps it was in J.R.R. Tolkien's book.

After emailing Jasper to ask for advice on cracking
codes, Harper started a spreadsheet listing the mini
mysteries linked to extinction. If she added in the lynx
mystery, now solved, there were eleven.

1. The Order of Dragons Mystery
2. The Disappearing Dragon Card Mystery
3. The Coded Conversation Mystery
4. The Father and Son Mystery
5. The Mystery of Who Bought Ollie Merriweather Lobster and Champagne
6. The Mystery of Who Blew Up the Cliff
7. The Mystery of Who Killed Johnny Roswell
8. The Mystery of the Man in the Blue Laces
9. The Mystery of Patient X
10. The Bluefin Tuna Mystery
11. The Mystery of the Stolen Iberian Lynx

Three remained.

12. The Mystery of the Intruder on the Roof
13. The Mystery of the Phantom Bodyguard
14. The Mystery of Why the Swanns Are in Bluebell Bay

Then she noticed something interesting. Seven of the mysteries were also connected to Hamilton Park. That got her thinking about the Order of Dragons, whose members were said to be rich and powerful politicians, businessmen, celebrities, and judges—exactly the sort of people who visited Hamilton Park.

Freya had described how Sir Haslemere, one of

Britain's wealthiest men, had insisted on having dozens of clocks ticking and blinking in his room during his stay, even though he was recovering from an operation on his last visit and needed his sleep. Yet each morning, he'd appeared at breakfast "looking as if he'd spent a month at a health spa."

What if the reason he was so fanatical about punctuality was because he had to take dragon's teeth tonic at precisely noon and midnight every day?

What if *Sir Haslemere* was Patient X? He'd been staying at Hamilton Park on the day she'd overheard the coded conversation. Could he have been the person buying Blue-Shoelace Man's tiger skins and ivory?

FaceTime trilled on her phone. Harper nearly had a heart attack when Kai's name came up. Was he telepathic?

His dimples and glasses sharpened into focus. "I have a confession," Kai began.

"Never a great opener," Harper said drily, propping her phone against the arm of the sofa.

Bailey pecked at the screen, startling Kai. "'I'm getting cuter by the minute!'" he shrieked. "'Cuter by the minute!'"

Harper put him on her shoulder. "What's this confession?"

"If I tell you, you have to promise not to hate me."

"Even if you've made everything up and there was

never any tall, dark stranger with blue laces wanting dragon's teeth—"

"All of that's true," said Kai.

"Then the worst that'll happen is I might hang up and never speak to you again," Harper said cheerfully.

"That's what I'm afraid of, but I won't be able to live with myself if you don't know the truth." Kai took a deep breath. "Okay, here goes. My dad blew up the cliff."

"What cliff?" said Harper. "Ohhh—*the* cliff."

"The Jurassic Dragon cliff, yes. And before you judge him, he did it for me," Kai said defensively. "Dad put himself through medical school working on a construction site, so he knows about explosives. He also knew how to get hold of them and how to detonate them remotely. With our fossils running low, he decided that the only way to get more dinosaur bones was to find them himself. So he hired a camouflage kayak . . ."

That solves that mystery, thought Harper.

". . . and worked out every detail—the tide, the weather, when the beach would be closed, and where to do it so nobody would get hurt. He'd rehearsed it the day before and chosen the exact spots he'd need to target in order to set off a landslide. Everything went to plan until he triggered the second explosive from his kayak. At that moment, he saw some kid playing with a dog on the cliff."

Kat, Harper thought incredulously. *He saw Kat.* "What did he do?"

"He yelled at them to get off the cliff, but it was already collapsing, and the waves capsized his kayak. He almost drowned. He did see the kid scramble to safety, but he was pretty messed up when he got back to London. As a doctor, he's taken an oath to save lives. But by trying to save my life, he'd almost killed someone else's child. The worst part was it was all for nothing. He never got his hands on a single fossil. The next morning, your dad found the dracoraptor, and the whole world descended upon Bluebell Bay."

On-screen, Harper watched Kai take off his glasses and polish them nervously.

"Are you going to give up on us, now that you know that my father could have killed some kid, or destroyed the Jurassic Dragon your father has spent years hunting for?"

Harper debated whether to explain about Kat and Pax but decided there wasn't enough time. "Of course we're not going to give up on you, and definitely not after you've been brave enough to tell the truth. No one would blame your dad for doing what he did. Kat and I are going to keep trying our best to identify members of the Order of Dragons. If we can do that, we might also find Patient X."

She brought Kai up to speed on their investigation,

pinging him links to the photos of Lucian Rigley and Sir Haslemere. "Could Lucian be the masked man who came to your father's practice?"

Kai frowned. "Hard to tell from a headshot. He looks as scary as the stranger sounded, but I couldn't say for sure."

"What about Sir Haslemere? Could he be Patient X?"

"No way," said Kai. "The photo you sent over was taken last week. He's much too healthy."

Harper was starting to despair. With every step forward, they took five back.

"Where's Kat?" Kai was asking. "Do you think she'd forgive us for this cliff business?"

"'Course she would. She was here earlier, grooming Ethan Swann's horse."

"You're kidding? That's so cool. I read about Ethan being in Bluebell Bay. I'm a massive fan of his."

Harper was astonished. "You are?"

"He does all his own stunts, you know. Ever seen *The Warrior's Way*? He plays this college football star whose career is ended by a car accident. He goes to a kung fu master in the mountains to learn to walk again. My favorite scene is where he does a running leap off a building. You think he can't possibly survive, but next he's rappelling down the side. Ethan spent a year in China training for the part."

And just like that, Harper connected the dots.

She pulled up the spreadsheet on her laptop. The only mystery she hadn't yet linked to *Extinction* or *Hamilton Park* was the question of why the Swanns were in Bluebell Bay.

If the couple were the glamorous holidaymakers they made out they were, there *was* no mystery. But if they'd come to Bluebell Bay for the Jurassic Dragon (i.e., *Extinction*), the picture changed dramatically.

It was impossible to believe that a Hollywood actor would drive all the way to Buckinghamshire to steal the paintings of Kat's dour foxhunting ancestors. If it was him using his kung fu skills on the roof of Hamilton Park, why was he there? To snatch a rare ivory carving from the man with blue laces? Or could he be an undercover spy or assassin, there to target the minister of defense? After all, it was the Dark Lord's bodyguard who'd fought the intruder off. And the following day, Ethan had greeted Kat with a black eye and a swollen cheek.

Great look for a movie actor, huh? he'd joked, blaming it on an "argument with the corner of the wardrobe."

Then something else occurred to Harper. What if Kat's grandfather was already investigating the possibility of a ring of illegal wildlife thieves under his roof? He loved animals as much as she and Kat did, and yet he hadn't responded to Kat's message about the overheard conversation about illegal wildlife products. That was curious, unless of course it gave him more evidence to act to stop Lucian Rigley. Maybe the reason the Order of Dragons had sent Ethan to Hamilton Park was because the Dark Lord was getting too close for comfort. Maybe they wanted him eliminated.

"I can't find any information on whether Lucian Rigley is tall or short," reported Kai, who'd been scrolling through government websites. "The masked man was at least two meters tall."

"Wow, that's nearly seven feet," Harper said. "Kai, do you know anything about code breaking? I have a theory that Johnny Roswell left some trace of his investigation somewhere—maybe even using *The Hobbit* to create a cipher." She held up the hardback.

Kai squinted at it. "Was he a tech wizard?"

"I doubt it."

"Then he might have used an old-fashioned hiding place. Check the flaps. He could have slipped a piece of paper under the inside cover and glued it down."

The flaps were stuck fast, but Kai had given Harper an idea. She fetched a torch and shone it down the hollow between the cover and the spine. Inside, a USB flash drive gleamed like a pearl.

"Kai, you just might be a genius. We've hit the jackpot, I think. I hope."

A cushion chirruped. Harper lifted it to discover Kat's forgotten phone. A message lit the screen.

Me again, honey. Tina and I have been called out to a foaling emergency. Back around 4 p.m.—in time to greet Tiny and Pax!

If Kat had cycled straight home, Dr. Wolfe would have seen her by now. Where was she?

Before Harper could decide what to do, she noticed another unread text. It must have come in, unheard, while the parrot was shrieking. Her stomach gave a queasy flip. The message was from herself, Harper. Since she knew for a fact that she hadn't texted Kat that day, she clicked on it.

Hey, Kat. I'm at Starfish Cove, and I've twisted my ankle. I can't get hold of my dad, and I need help urgently. Please hurry!

Harper dropped the phone as if she'd been electrocuted. She knew now how Johnny had been lured to disaster two years ago by the Order of Dragons— with a cloned phone number just like this one.

By all accounts, the young nature writer had been a loyal friend. If his buddy had texted him saying that he'd twisted his ankle and needed help, Johnny would have rushed to his aid immediately. He'd have been scrambling around the wet, fragile cliffs searching for Harry, who was safely indoors, oblivious to what was happening. When the landslide happened, the monsters who orchestrated it would have been miles away from the scene.

Harper was beside herself with fear for Kat's safety, but in a panic about how best to help her. Nettie was away in Somerset, and Professor Lamb had called earlier to say his train was delayed. She could ring the police, but not even Sergeant Singh would believe her. She was on her own.

Or was she?

"Harper, what's happened?" Kai asked anxiously from her screen. "You look as if you've seen an ender dragon circling."

"Someone's texted Kat from a clone account, pretending to be me. She isn't here, so she hasn't received it, but whoever sent it may have a backup plan. Kai, I'm positive she's in danger."

Kai didn't hesitate. "Tell me how to help, and I'll do it. Should I ring emergency services?"

"No, ring this number and ask for Lord Hamilton-Crosse. Tell him Kat's in trouble. Tell him to send urgent help to Starfish Cove."

Fat drops of rain splattered Harper's bare arms as she ran through the orchard. The cherry trees squeaked and strained in the gale.

"The things I do for you, Kat Wolfe," she muttered out loud in the vain hope that Kat's easy courage and horse-whispering skills might settle on her shoulders like fairy dust. It didn't work. One look at the whites of Charming Outlaw's eyes and her nerve failed her. A trash can clattering around the yard had left him in a fever of agitation. He was snorting and sweating and spinning in his box.

Terror hit Harper like an ocean wave. She hadn't ridden the chestnut since she broke her legs falling off him, and she knew then that nothing would induce her to ride him now. Not even the thought of Kat in peril.

Orkaan chose that moment to arch her head over her stable door. Her black ears were pricked, her breathing regular. There was something imploring in her gaze, as if she yearned to be out galloping in the stormy weather she was named for, as if she was longing to show that she could be bold and daring too. A bloom of courage swelled inside Harper. With Orkaan's help, Mission: Impossible suddenly became Mission: Possible.

In record time, she was swinging Orkaan's Western saddle onto the mare's back, tightening the cinch and clambering aboard. The wind tore at Harper's jacket as they headed out of the yard, Orkaan's black mane flowing.

Charming Outlaw gave a piercing whinny, but Harper never looked around. As a consequence, she never saw a figure slip into the storeroom and take a bridle from a hook. Minutes later, Outlaw—and a new, strange rider—left the yard.

EVEN DRAGONS

"WHAT MAKES YOU THINK THAT XENA came down here?" asked Kat.

If wishes were horses, she'd have a herd. She wished she'd brought a sweater for starters. A cruel wind whipped at her T-shirt, making it hum. The heat of the past few days was a distant memory. She wished she'd checked about when the storm would be arriving too. The sky and sea had lost their friendly blue, and the waves were gun-barrel gray.

If only she'd cycled straight home, as she'd told Harper she would. Instead, she'd gone in search of Robyn. Passing the deli, she'd been surprised to see her new friend's sleeping bag on the step, together with a folded shirt and two mismatched socks.

Kat had done a double take. One had purple stripes.

Margo had emerged from the deli then. She'd

bundled up Robyn's belongings before she noticed Kat. "Sweetie, I'm so sorry for the misunderstanding on Monday. You did us all a favor, you know."

"I did?"

"You did," Margo said warmly. "In our zeal to make Bluebell Bay the perfect seaside town, we forgot that we once prided ourselves on welcoming strangers. When the Jurassic Dragon made us rich, we forgot how to be openhearted. It took you, a slip of girl, to remind us. Er, have you seen Robyn? I want a word with her."

"I thought you were going to be more welcoming," Kat accused.

"Oh, I am. It's just that ever since Robyn stopped vandals from destroying a historic statue one day and put a notorious shoplifter in an armlock the next, she's become so popular that the shopkeepers are squabbling over her. Everyone wants her to guard their business."

She glanced at the scudding black clouds. "I do hope she comes back before the storm hits. I thought I'd bring in her sleeping bag, just in case. Not, I suppose, that she'd care. I offered her the room above my deli rent-free in return for her keeping an eye on the place at night. You won't believe what she said. *Thanks, but I don't do walls.*"

V doesn't do walls.

Kat had started to laugh.

"What's funny?" bristled Margo.

"Nothing. If you see Robyn, would you mind telling her I'm looking for her?"

"Will do." Margo paused on the step. "You'll be sorry, no doubt, to say goodbye to that ginger menace and your starry clients."

"What ginger menace?"

"Alicia Swann's Pomeranian. Haven't you heard? The Swanns are leaving town. Better hurry if you want to catch them."

Kat had pedaled furiously in the direction of the hotel, wondering why the actors hadn't told her they were checking out. Surely they weren't planning to skip town without paying their pet-sitting bill. She didn't mind so much about her own fee. She had a soft spot for Xena, and taking care of Orkaan had been pure pleasure. But she'd object very strongly if the Swanns absconded without reimbursing the Lambs for the hay, horse feed, and broken bridle.

As she rode, Kat's head swirled with the revelation that V and Robyn were one and the same person. Had her grandfather sent his "phantom" bodyguard to protect her because he was concerned about unscrupulous Jurassic Dragon hunters in Bluebell Bay? Or had V come on a mission of her own?

Lost in thought, she'd very nearly crashed into a ragamuffin of a boy. He'd popped up in front of her, making airplane arms.

"Are you the pet-sitter kid? That actress, Alicia Swann, needs your help. She's freaking out because she's lost her dog on the coastal path."

Now, Kat wished she'd paused to ask, "Why me? Why not you or Ethan or the emergency services?" but all she thought about was the miniature Pomeranian being blown out to sea as a gale moved in.

It was only when she skidded to a halt that she realized she'd left her phone at Paradise House. That meant she couldn't tell her mum where she was or ask if she or Tina could assist with the search of Starfish Cove, a place so secret that even the Jurassic Dragon crowds had failed to discover it.

Instead, she sensed she'd soon have the answer to the question she'd been wanting to ask since the Swanns arrived in Bluebell Bay.

Which of their many faces was the real one?

"What makes you think Xena came down here?" asked Kat, staring at the path that wiggled down to Starfish Cove. In a weak moment, she'd told the actress about her favorite bay, revealed to her by Edith on condition that she never speak of it to anyone but Harper. But Alicia had been looking for a private sunbathing spot, and somehow Kat had found herself recommending it with the enthusiasm of a travel agent.

Alicia was a wreck. Beneath her black baseball cap,

her eyes were puffy with crying and her usually blemish-free skin was a mottled maroon. Twice she staggered, as if she might faint. Kat wished again that she had her phone in case they had to call a doctor. Alicia did not look well at all.

"Sorry, Kat—it's this wretched cold. I can't seem to shake it. My husband and I came to Bluebell Bay for a vacation, but we've had one disaster after another. I'm sure Xena cursed us by digging up that stupid skull. Why, only yesterday, a clumsy maid at the Majestic broke my bottle of herbal tonic, the only thing that makes me feel better. Now we're leaving, and I won't have time to get another."

Kat was shocked to hear poor Johnny dismissed as a curse, but she attributed it to the stress of losing Xena and to Alicia's cold, which had fogged up her brain. "My friend Mario Rossi has a drawer full of herbal tonics in his motor home at the campground near Durdle Door. I could ask him if you like."

Kat did now think of Mario as a friend, and had even had a chance to ask him about the picture. His coasteering instructor had found the kayak washed up on the shore near Durdle Door. No one had come forward to claim it.

Alicia rallied at the mention of Mario's herbal medicine stash. "Do you think Mario might sell me one or two? Maybe Ethan and I could swing by the campsite on the way out of town. We've left your money at the front desk, by the way. You didn't think we'd leave without paying, did you, Kat?"

"No, Mrs. Swann. Thanks, Mrs. Swann." Kat was relieved. Alicia was a good person, after all.

All the same, she felt uneasy about being out on the cliffs with a megastar she didn't entirely trust in such an isolated place. The gale was moving in faster than expected, and nobody knew where she was. So she did the only thing she could think of. "Any chance you could autograph my notebook very quickly, Mrs. Swann? My friends at school are huge fans, but they'll never believe I was your pet sitter if I don't have something to prove it."

"Love to, darling," said Alicia unenthusiastically, "but I don't have a pen."

"I do!" Kat took the Pi-Craft recorder from her rucksack and surreptitiously pressed record.

"Cool pen," commented Alicia, scrawling in Kat's notebook: *Thanks, Kat Wolfe, World's Best Pet Sitter. Love, Alicia Swann.*

"Keep it." Kat said airily, knowing that the recording would automatically upload to a cloud account. "Where did you last see Xena?"

"I'm not sure. I've been wandering around in a daze. To be truthful, Ethan and I had words. I came here to clear my head before the long drive back to London. I didn't think it would hurt to let Xena off the leash, but she was gone in the blink of an eye. She's just so darn independent . . . Did you just hear a yelp? I think that might have been her."

Still clutching the pen and notebook, Alicia hurtled away down the high-sided path. Kat followed rather resentfully. She loathed being separated from her case notes—the lists of suspects and lines of inquiry—she'd detailed in her notebook.

And something else was bothering her. If the Swanns had the money to rent the best horse Pet Performers had to offer, while staying in an ocean-view suite and driving a silver Aston Martin, why couldn't they pay their pet sitter nine measly pounds each time she walked their dog or groomed their horse? Why had they left it till the last minute to settle their bill? She only had Alicia's word that they'd left any money at all.

Was it because the Swanns, like the queen, never carried cash? Or were they actually broke? Had they run up huge debts hiring sports cars and staying in luxury spas around the world? Or did their money go somewhere else? Somewhere more sinister?

A salty gust of wind almost knocked Kat off her feet. Far below, the sea was snake green and streaked with white. It was beautiful in a frightening sort of way. Above the roar of waves, Kat heard a faint whimper.

"There she is!" she cried, spotting the tiny Pomeranian.

Xena was shivering at the edge of the cliff, just meters from the path. Her collar was caught on a twisted root. A nearby pillar of sandstone had shielded her from the worst of the wind. Kat's stomach gave a lurch. The Pomeranian was in a position almost identical to that of Pax on the day of the cliff collapse. It was eerie.

"Xena, how do you get yourself into these scrapes?" scolded Alicia in a loving tone. "We're going to rescue you—aren't we, Kat?" As she looked around, the light caught her eyes.

The whites were mustard yellow.

There's cosmetic stuff they can do to hide it in the early stages, Kai had said about Patient X's condition. *But it won't last long.*

Time slowed. Kat felt as if she were watching herself from a great height. If there was even a one-in-a-million chance that Alicia was a member of the Order of Dragons and knew that she and Harper had been investigating their secret empire, Kat's survival would depend upon what she did next. She had to out-act an Oscar-winning actress.

She'd passed only two tourists on the way, and they'd been taking a selfie and hadn't noticed her. Rather than locking her bike, she'd shoved it under a bush to save time. If she never made it back, it could be days before anyone found it.

She remembered Ethan standing in the flower bed

at Paradise House, prattling on about the "magic" dinosaur. Kat hadn't heard his Aston Martin arrive because nobody was meant to. She supposed he must have turned off the engine and pushed the car down the sloping lane. Could the actor have been staking out the place—perhaps planning a smash-and-grab raid of what he'd thought was the real Jurassic Dragon skeleton on the table?

Film stars lived and died by their looks. If anyone was likely to pay any price or try any snake oil for the promise of health and eternal youth, it was the Swanns. But would they go so far as to be members of the Order of Dragons? Was it really possible that Alicia Swann, who just a week before had looked traffic-stoppingly beautiful, was Patient X?

"I'm going to run for help," she told Alicia. "The cliff edges around here crumble easily, especially if it's been raining. It's too risky for us to try to reach Xena. We're going to need the fire department or coast guard. I won't be long."

"Help? We don't need any help, not with Xena practically within touching distance. You're as light as a feather. Just pick her up, and you'll be back on the path in a flash. That cliff's been standing for millennia. Why would it fall today?"

Kat felt ill. She'd blithely thought the exact same thing as she clambered down to rescue Pax. Moments later, they'd fight for their lives. She really didn't want a repeat of that little adventure.

Xena let out a heartrending whine.

"Hang in there, my little warrior princess," cooed Alicia, casting a tearful look at Kat. "I hope we'll be able to save you."

Kat wanted more than anything to run away as fast as her legs could carry her, but she'd never leave an animal in trouble, and she knew that Alicia knew that.

The ground the Pomeranian was standing on looked firm enough. The quicker she rescued Xena, the quicker she could escape. "All right, I'll go."

Alicia clapped her hands like a child. "Kat, you're a superstar. Careful now."

No one in history had ever untangled a leash from a twisted root faster than Kat. Snatching up Xena, she picked her way through the scrub to solid ground. She was halfway back before she realized that Alicia wasn't watching them. She was reading Kat's notebook.

Wind ruffled the pages. Mario Rossi's key card fell out. The actress caught it in midair. "What's this?"

"The entry key for Mario's motor home."

Kat set down the dog and reached for the card, but the actress shoved it into her pocket. "Is this your journal? Do you keep a diary of your adventures or write poems or dreams? That's what I did when I was your age." She began to flick through Kat's case notes.

"Hey, that's private!"

Kat made a grab for the notebook, but Alicia held it out of range. "*The Mystery of Why the Swanns Are in Bluebell Bay*? *The Order of Dragons Mystery*? My, you've been busy, Kat Wolfe. Lucian told me that you and your little friend fancied yourselves junior private eyes, but I didn't believe him. He'd heard about a spy whose mission you ruined. So, what did you come up with? Why *are* Ethan and I in Bluebell Bay?"

She took a step in Kat's direction. Kat moved back.

"We were just playing around—playing at being detectives. I'm sorry. It doesn't mean anything. Please give it to me."

"Playing around? You really think you can get off that easily?"

Rain speckled Kat's upturned face. The storm was almost upon them. "Mrs. Swann—Alicia—Xena's been through a lot. We should get her back to the hotel before we all get drenched. We can talk there. As long as you pay the Lambs for the horse feed and bridle, I don't care about my fee."

Alicia laughed. "There *is* no fee because there *is* no money. Have you any clue how much it costs to look this good? Finding the rarest fossils from the remotest corners of the Far East or Bluebell Bay or wherever doesn't come cheap. That's why our society—I see you know about the Order of Dragons—that's why we're banking on extinction. We're filling bank vaults with tiger skins, rhino horn, and ivory. When wild tigers, rhinos, and elephants are gone, we'll be rich beyond our wildest dreams."

Banking on extinction.

In that second, Kat knew why Johnny had kept the stories on bluefin tuna. He'd been planning to tell the world about the "monsters" who saw wild creatures as gold.

At Hamilton Park, Lucian Rigley wasn't trading in rhino horn because he believed it could help arthritis. He was helping the Order of Dragons push endangered animals toward extinction so that their skins and bones shot up in value. The Dragons would then use that fortune to pay for the dinosaur tonics that they hoped would cure their illnesses and prolong their lives.

Kat was shivering with the shock of it all. "But what about me and my generation? Don't you care about us? We want to grow up and see elephants and tigers in the wild. We want oceans to be alive with whales and dolphins and tuna."

"That's because you're young and healthy," said Alicia wearily. "One day, you'll realize that youth and beauty are more important than any number of tigers."

The gale was moaning like a beast in pain, and the

afternoon sky had darkened to violet. Xena whined. Kat longed to pick her up but didn't dare. Alicia advanced, forcing Kat backward.

Kat knew she was perilously close to the edge of the cliff. She had to keep talking in the hope of bringing Alicia to her senses.

"Has it been worth it, Alicia—or should I call you Patient X? That is you, isn't it? After all the lying and stealing, the dragon's teeth tonic has failed. Admit it. You're sick. Let's get to the hotel and call an ambulance. You should be in the hospital."

Alicia's eyes filled with tears, and for a moment Kat thought she'd touched a nerve. But that, like everything else, was an act.

"Sorry, Kat—there's too much at stake. This was never meant to happen. We only wanted to take what was ours—our piece of the Jurassic Dragon. But you couldn't let it go, could you? You and Harper had to keep digging. You're almost as bad as the minister of defense. Someday soon, we'll be rid of him too."

Perhaps it was the menace in her voice or the threatening move she made toward Kat. Either way, it was too much for the Pomeranian. She flew at her mistress and bit her ankle. Alicia lashed out at the dog, but Xena was already bounding into Kat's arms.

There was a shout. Kat and Alicia looked up. Harper

and Orkaan were leaning over a precipice above them, a blur in the quickening rain. As fate would have it, at that exact moment, a jagged line appeared in the sandstone at Kat's feet. The cliff was beginning to collapse.

Not again, thought Kat. But before she could panic, a rope came tumbling down toward her.

"Tie this around you!" yelled Harper. "Don't worry—we'll pull you up."

When Robyn—code name V—came racing through the gale on Charming Outlaw, Harper was already directing the black mare to raise Kat to safety.

"Back, Orkaan," Harper was saying authoritatively as the Friesian's muscles bunched and strained. "Good girl. Back. Easy now."

Robyn was just in time to grab Kat's arms and help haul her to safety. "Your grandfather sent me to Bluebell Bay to watch over you and protect you, but it looks as if Harper's already got it covered. Now that you're okay, would you mind holding my—*your*—horse? I have an appointment with a dragon."

She sprinted back along the coastal path. The racehorse had clipped Alicia with his shoulder as she'd veered out of the rain, her skin jaundiced, her ankle bloody. Frantic to reach Kat before it was too late, V had left the actress lying on the ground. Now she headed back toward her. But though a black baseball cap and designer tracksuit top were still on the path—crumpled and sodden in the downpour, their owner was nowhere to be seen.

Like a dragon throwing off its plumage or a snake shedding its skin, Alicia Swann was gone.

TROUBLE IN PARADISE

Côte d'Azur, France

IN THE DECADE HE'D WORKED FOR THE most legendary hotel in Cannes, Francois Boursier had seen everything. Billionaires by the dozen. So many dazzling award-winning actresses that his pulse barely stirred at the sight of them. Singers, sportsmen, and supermodels. Presidents and reality TV stars. Sooner or later, they all checked in to the Carlton.

Then there were the lesser-known guests, such as the widow signing the hotel register now with a liver-spotted hand clumsy with jewels. Beneath the broad brim of her hat, she had a faded glamour, as if she'd once had Hollywood looks before too much sun and rich food had caught up with her.

"*Merci*, Madame Pemberton. Here is your key. Eduardo will show you to your room."

The bellman lifted her leopard-print tote bag and

was startled by the weight of it. It clinked as he lifted it onto the trolley.

"Careful!" she said sharply.

The glare she shot him caused the joke he was about to make about the bag containing a crate of champagne or a baby elephant to shrivel in his throat. After showing her to her suite, Eduardo left without waiting for a tip.

Once he'd gone, Madame Pemberton, alias Alicia Swann, went to the window. The Mediterranean Sea was a peacock blue. She'd driven through the night from the Jurassic Coast to France's Côte d'Azur, stopping only to collect a fake passport and change into one of the many disguises she'd left in a storage facility.

It was boiling in the "rich widow" costume, especially on a blazing-hot day. She'd have done anything to go down to the beach club for a dip, but that wouldn't be possible for a while. But someday soon, she'd build a new empire. Extinction would always be profitable.

Later, she planned to have a glass of fizz in Le Grand Salon to celebrate getting away with it. It had been a close-run thing. She'd underestimated that pet-sitter brat and her friend. And who could have foreseen that the homeless woman would come bearing down on her like a Valkyrie? It was a pity she'd never again see Xena or Ethan, whom she'd glimpsed being pushed into a police car in handcuffs, perhaps due to the unpaid hotel bill, but neither of them were worth a spell in a jail cell. She was free as a bird and intended to remain that way.

First, though, she needed a nap.

As she settled between the inviting cream sheets of the queen-sized bed, she noticed a python-skin cushion propped against the pillows. It was an odd choice for such an elegant hotel, but Alicia heartily approved of rare animal skins as home accessories. Another creature wiped from the Earth could only be a good thing for her bank balance. Collapsing onto the bed, she shut her eyes and flung out her arms.

Until that moment, Mr. B had enjoyed his adventure. Before fleeing Bluebell Bay, Alicia had used the dragon key card taken from Kat to sneak into Mario's motor home and steal his herbal tonics. While she was helping herself to a bottle of sparkling water from his fridge, Mr. B had slithered into her tote bag. He'd dozed contentedly among her jars and soft scarves as Alicia raced from Dorset to Dover, and from Calais to the Côte d'Azur. Apart from a bout of queasiness during the ferry crossing, he'd had fun.

But he hadn't appreciated being booted in the belly by the bellman (who'd given the bag a kick out of spite), and he certainly didn't like being clouted in the head by Alicia Swann as she lay down beside him. Panicking, he flung a cool tail over her stomach. When she screeched at the top of her lungs and began bashing him with her fists, he had no option but to bind her wrists together with his coils. At that stage, she'd fainted.

During the struggle, her wig came off, along with a chunk of her rubbery mask. Hearing the commotion, hotel security burst into the room, followed by a chambermaid. When the maid caught sight of the python, she promptly passed out beside Alicia.

The gendarme who attended the exotic scene shortly afterward said it was the first time he'd ever heard of a snake performing a citizen's arrest.

EPILOGUE

Six Weeks Later
Soarsa Wilderness Reserve,
Scottish Highlands

"IS EVERYONE COMFORTABLE?" ASKED Lord Hamilton-Crosse. "Does anyone need a blanket? Have you had enough to eat? If not, I've brought—"

"Please, no more food," begged Kat. "The wild mushroom stew at the lodge was so yummy that I had two portions with the hot potato scones before anyone told me we'd be toasting vegan coconut marshmallows . . ."

"At least you didn't eat ten," groaned Harper, clutching her stomach.

"This is the first time I've heard either of you complain about too much food," remarked Dr. Wolfe. "Too little, on the other hand . . ."

Kat laughed and turned to the man on the bench beside her. "We're definitely not complaining. Thanks, Grandfather. It's been perfect."

"It has," agreed Harper. "Thank you for organizing it, sir."

"It's been unforgettable, Lord Hamilton-Crosse," added Kai.

To which His Lordship responded, "Dirk would be fine, thanks, Kai."

Two nights earlier, Dr. Wolfe, Kat, Harper, and Kai had boarded the Caledonian Sleeper for the Highlands of Scotland. Kat had fallen asleep to a click-clack of rails and woken as the train wound past a mountain wreathed in pink cotton candy cloud. She and Harper had lain on their bunks watching storybook forests slide by.

At Gleneagles station, they'd been met by Graeme, a flame-bearded man in a kilt. He'd whisked them along nerve-shredding bends to Soarsa Wilderness Lodge, where Kat's grandfather was waiting. "*Soarsa* is Gaelic for 'freedom' or 'liberty,'" Graeme told them. "We feel quite strongly about that here in the Land of the Brave."

One breath of the mint-fresh air had supercharged Kat's lungs. Hiking across moors ablaze with purple heather and yellow gorse had done the same for her spirit. And that evening, they'd exchanged a log fire at the lodge for a pine-scented wildlife hide.

Kai was staring dreamily out at a silver lake ringed by pines. Kat knew he was wishing his father was with him. Dr. Liu had stayed behind to give evidence to Scotland

Yard detectives, who were working with MI5 to round up the leaders of the Order of Dragons.

Professor Lamb, meanwhile, was working with Natural History Museum experts to move the dracoraptor from Dorset to London, where it would be safe from bone thieves. The Jurassic Dragon was going to be officially named *Dracoraptor agnus* (Dragon lamb) after the professor's discovery.

Assisting with the dinosaur's move was Harry Holt, the newest member of Theo Lamb's team. He'd been cleared of all charges and praised by the minister of defense and Sergeant Singh for keeping Johnny's USB flash drive safe, even though he'd never been able to open the investigation it detailed. He'd always blamed himself after Johnny went missing, fearing that Johnny either had met with an accident while out fossil hunting or had been harmed by the Order of Dragons—the secretive society Harry had encouraged him to expose.

Alicia Swann, aka Patient X, was in a French hospital under armed guard. She was not expected to survive long enough to stand trial.

"It's a pity that she won't face justice—not in this life, at least," Kat's grandfather had told the girls. "But thanks to Johnny's investigation, the voice recording on Kat's pen, Wolfe and Lamb Incorporated's peerless detective work, and clever Mr. Bojangles, Alicia's fellow Dragons *will* be prosecuted.

"It's ironic that it took an adventurous python to bring down one of the most elusive fossil and wildlife criminals in history. Had Mr. B not caused Alicia to scream so loudly that she brought hotel security, it's likely that she'd have slipped the net and taken the names of Lucian—your blue-shoelaces man—and her other accomplices to the grave. Not even Ethan had access to her little black book. He was a committed Dragon, as obsessed with preserving his youth and looks as she was. But in reality, she was the brains."

"But didn't she love him?" asked Harper.

"I'm sure she did—in her way," said the Dark Lord, "but it seemed he angered her and the rest of the Dragons when he failed to assassinate me." He grimaced. "Yes, that's what he was doing on the roof of Hamilton Park—a fight I gather you saw. Thankfully, V's Mongoose moves chased him off."

"Leaping Tiger," murmured Kat.

"Leaping Tiger, yes. Not something I want you trying at home," he said sternly.

Kat hastily changed the subject. "What about Mr. B? Who's taking care of him?"

"Happily, the gendarme who arrested Alicia is a reptile expert who'll give Mr. B an excellent home until Mario can collect him. Any news on Alicia's Pomeranian?"

Kat smiled. "She's been adopted by a dog-mad kid I

met in the caravan park. Xena'll have a lovely life with Immie and her mum. So will Pax—with you."

Giving up the border collie had been one of the hardest things Kat had ever done, but at Summer Street, Pax would have spent a lot of time shut indoors while Kat was at school and Dr. Wolfe was working. So Kat had approached her grandfather, who, as she'd suspected, was already besotted with the collie. Pax would have a glorious life at Hamilton Park, taking long walks with His Lordship and helping James and Flush with the sheep.

Even better, Tiny would continue to rule the roost at Summer Street.

"It's great that the Dragons are being rounded up," Harper said to Kat's grandfather, "but do you think you'll ever win the fight against wildlife crime? As soon as one dragon is slain, doesn't another pop up somewhere else?"

"Sadly, yes."

"You're saying there's no hope!" cried Kat.

He smiled. "Actually, I believe the opposite. There's oceans of hope. We'll win when we understand that everything's connected. You, Harper, and Kai are proof of that. You came together to overcome evil and help make our Earth a kinder, more beautiful place. Every lynx, tiger, tuna, or tree lost removes a brick from the wall of life. But every one saved puts it back."

Kai looked unsure. "Is that really possible?"

Dr. Wolfe leaned forward. "Let me tell you a story, Kai. Some years ago, wolves were reintroduced to Yellowstone Park in America after a seventy-year absence. Conservationists knew that they might hunt some deer, but what they didn't expect was what came next.

"First, the deer began to spread out around the park for safety. Without the deer to chew the vegetation to stumps, the forests flourished. The songbirds returned, and the beavers began to build dams, which helped fish, reptiles, and otters to thrive. The wolves also reduced the number of coyotes, which meant more rabbits and rodents, which in turn brought more hawks and bald eagles. The bear population rose because fewer deer meant more berries, and the thicker vegetation stopped erosion, so the rivers meandered less. The wolves changed the landscape—for the better."

"Wolves move rivers," Kai said wonderingly.

The Dark Lord's watch flashed red. He was on his feet at once, saying his goodbyes. Kat followed him outside.

"Rabbit under the fence again? Or is it a situation?"

He laughed. "A situation. Sorry—I have to fly. Promise you'll visit Pax, Faith, and your ancient grandfather at Hamilton Park very soon."

"You're not ancient," Kat said loyally. "And yes, I promise." A movement in the pines caught her eye. In the purple shadows, a rider waited with two horses.

Her grandfather hugged her. "Until the next time, young Kat. Remember, even dragons have their ending."

Kat laughed. "I'm not likely to forget."

She watched him fade into the twilight with V, whose life he'd saved many years before, and who'd since devoted every waking hour to doing the same for him.

Kai leaned out of the hide. "Kat, come quickly. It's happening."

Inside, Kat sat between him and Harper, barely breathing as a lynx, *her lynx*, crept out of the pines and padded down to the water's edge.

"Forget video games," whispered Kai. "*This* is what I want to do with my life: become a guardian of the wild. Only I'm going to do it by becoming a doctor like my dad. I'll fight to save endangered animals from the inside by showing patients ways to feel better that are good for everyone, including the planet."

The deep velvet dark of the Scottish Highlands had descended like a theater curtain. Soon, Kat was no longer sure where the wildcat ended and the pines and mountains began, but the impression of her—proud, innocent, and part of the ancient landscape—remained.

"*You* and your mum helped Mario to save the lynx from the hunters and bring her to this special, peaceful place," Harper said later as she and Kat sat stargazing out the bedroom window. "So it's not only wolves that move rivers. Wolfes do it too."

Kat grinned. "Yes, but we'll always need a Lamb to help us. And now we have Kai as a Wolfe and Lamb detective agency deputy to add to Edith, our champion researcher. We're a crack team. Next time we have a mystery to solve, we'll be a force to reckon with."

"Do you think there'll be a next time?" Harper asked hopefully.

"I know there will. Wolfe and Lamb forever, right?"

They bumped fists in the darkness, and Harper felt a rush of joy. Soon—very soon—they'd be detectives again. "Wolfe and Lamb forever," she echoed.

It may have been coincidence, but as she spoke, a shooting star sparkled across the sky. The lynx, which was climbing a crag, paused to watch it before continuing on up the mountain, her ears attuned to danger, her big paws treading lightly on the earth.

Free.

ACKNOWLEDGMENTS

Perhaps because it's about the subject closest to my heart, *Kat Wolfe Takes the Case* was one of the hardest novels I've ever written. All books take a village, but this time that felt especially true. As long as I write, I'll never forget the kindness, patience, and support over the past year of Venetia Gosling, my editor at Macmillan; Catherine Clarke, my agent at Felicity Bryan Associates; and Wes Adams, my editor at Farrar Straus Giroux. Thank you all so, so much. This book wouldn't have happened without you.

I'd been a journalist and written a fair few books on a fair few subjects before I became a children's author, and I'm grateful every day for the very wonderful children's book community. Special thanks go to Katherine Rundell, Abi Elphinstone, and Piers Torday for providing wise counsel, company, and just pure joy exactly when all those things were most needed. The next dinner is on me!

For dracoraptor advice, I'm indebted to Dr. Ben Garrod. I take full responsibility for any paleontological errors or leaps of fantasy, particularly with regard to the moving of the Jurassic Dragon! All dinosaur errors are mine alone.

Huge thanks to designer Aimee Fleck and artist Vivienne To for the stunning cover, and to the lovely, super-talented team at FSG/Macmillan Kids, especially Melissa Warten, Lindsay Wagner, and copy editor Erica Ferguson.

Of course, none of this would be possible or half as much fun without the love and support of my friends Merina, Emelia, Jean, and Jane; and my family, Jules, Lisa, and my mum and dad.

Last but not least, thank you for the many dedicated and just plain brilliant booksellers at Waterstones and incredible indies such as Octavia's Bookshop and Tales on Moon Lane. Thank you for every children's book you hand-sell every day. You make the world a better place.

HELP KAT AND HARPER STOP EXTINCTION

In *Kat Wolfe Takes the Case*, Kat, Harper, and Kai encounter extinction at every turn. Their case and my story are fiction, but the facts behind both are real.

Some bits of the book were drawn from personal experience. When I was Kat and Harper's age, our farmhouse in Zimbabwe was like an animal hospital. My family rescued everything from baby warthogs (we named them Miss Piggy and Bacon) to owls, lambs, calves, cats, dogs, a goat, and, best of all, a baby monkey.

When I was seventeen, I spent a year in the U.K. working as a veterinary nurse at an animal clinic. And now I'm an ambassador for the Born Free Foundation, which rescues lions, leopards, and tigers from horrific situations of captivity and rehomes them in a beautiful sanctuary for life.

In *Kat Wolfe Takes the Case,* Mr. B is based on a

python I kept briefly in Zimbabwe. Her name was Samantha, and she did in fact do her best to crush both my arms and would have bitten me had I not been saved by my dad. I had no difficulty putting myself in Kat's shoes!

Most other plotlines in the book are based on real events. All over the world, precious paleontological sites are being destroyed by unscrupulous "dragon's teeth" and dinosaur-bone thieves. They sell their wares to collectors and to the same dodgy practitioners who hawk rhino horn, pangolin scales, and seahorses to patients, claiming they can prolong life.

While I, personally, have trouble believing in the healing powers of fossils, I'm very much a fan of acupuncture and alternative medicine of all kinds and for a long time considered becoming a healer myself. When I was a child in Africa, plants such as aloe vera and the bark and fruit of trees such as the baobab and sausage tree (*Kigelia Africana*) were used by my own family and local people all the time. When I had third-degree burns, I was saved by manuka honey. But, like Kat, Kai, and Harper, I feel strongly that both prescribed and traditional medicine should help, not harm, the planet.

Heartbreakingly, there really are wealthy people and evil corporations who are banking on extinction, stockpiling ivory, tiger skins, lion bones, pangolin scales, and, yes, bluefin tuna, in the expectation that their value will shoot up once these creatures become extinct. They look at wild animals and see gold.

Many of these people would have you believe that because species such as tiger, rhino, and bluefin tuna can be farmed it's fine to use them as rugs or to make sushi. However, the reason a single bluefin tuna was sold for $3.3 million on the Tokyo fish market in January 2019 was because it was wild-caught. Those who use endangered animals as sushi or to cure ailments believe that the wildness of the animal is what gives these products flavor or potency. The wild creatures are the ones they want. They believe that eating or bottling wild animals can help them live longer.

They're dead wrong. Every human, tree, and animal on our planet is interconnected. If weed killer wipes out scores of bees in Australia or South America, or a tiny shrew goes extinct somewhere in Europe, chances are, you'll never know about it. But across the globe, the lives of scores of other people and animals will be directly impacted. The crops that were due to be exported might fail because there are no bees to pollinate them and the birds and creatures that might have fed on them might also be lost. A certain rare eagle that lived off the tiny shrew might be pushed to the brink of extinction because its only food source is now gone.

If we don't do everything in our power to save every bird, tree, and wild animal on the planet, we won't have a future.

With so many challenging issues facing our environment, it's easy to feel hopeless. My advice: Don't give into it. To paraphrase Kat's grandfather, hope—oceans of it—is everywhere. *You* give me hope. Yes, you, the reader of this book. If you've made it this far, chances are that you care about animals and nature. Chances are you want a better world.

Young people everywhere give me hope. So many incredible youngsters are fiercely intelligent, caring, and passionate about saving animals and the environment and keeping our earth kind and beautiful.

The good news is, you can help stop extinction in its tracks. You don't have to save the tiger or beluga whale all on your own. You can start with some of the species in your backyard or balcony. Here are a few tips.

1. Get engaged and get your friends involved. For inspiration, follow teen naturalists and activists Dara McAnulty or Bella Lack on Twitter or read Dara's award-winning blog: youngfermanaghnaturalist.wordpress.com.

2. Avoid products containing palm oil. The creation of oil palm plantations is devastating rain forests and the

chimpanzees, orangutans, birds, and other creatures that live in them.

3. Don't eat bluefin tuna, and avoid all tuna if possible. Most species are threatened or near-threatened. So-called line-caught tuna is not caught by a friendly fisherman on a beach with a rod but by ships trailing hundreds of lines, each loaded with up to two thousand hooks. Dolphins and sharks are decimated along with every catch.

4. Ditch single-use plastic. Our oceans are becoming plastic soup, killing tens of millions of birds, fish, and whales that swim with their mouths open to catch small fish and plankton. Carry reusable water bottles and coffee cups and encourage your school and parents to ban plastic bags, cups, and cutlery.

5. Say NO to dolphin and orca encounters. Everyone wants to swim with dolphins, but try to do it in the wild, where they at least have a choice about whether to stay or go. If you have any doubts about whether dolphins and orcas suffer in captivity, watch *Blackfish*, a documentary about the "entertainment" industry.

6. Eat less meat and dairy. Commercial farming is accelerating habitat loss, rain forest destruction, and global warming.

7. Adopt animals from shelters and sanctuaries. I rescued my Bengal cat, Max, from the Royal Society for the Protection of Cruelty to Animals (RSPCA), and he's repaid me with more love and joy than I could ever have imagined. He's my best friend.

8. Saving species is one of the most important jobs on earth right now. Get your family, friends, or school involved in helping birds, butterflies, bees, and other insects, which often get forgotten. Putting out nesting boxes, winter feed, and bee or insect hotels is vital, life-saving work.

9. In 2018, I launched an alliance of more than fifty children's authors called Authors4Oceans to campaign against the use of plastic in the book industry and in schools. Our website is packed with resources and cool blogs and tips on how you can help fight the plastic tide and save marine species. Follow us on Twitter or visit our website: authors4oceans.org.

10. I'm an ambassador for the Born Free Foundation and can wholeheartedly say they're one of the most extraordinary charities on earth. Find out how you can be involved here: bornfree.org.uk.